A Pride & Prejudice Epistolary

A
Proper
Introduction

ALIX JAMES

Book Cover by SelfPubBookCovers.com

Blog and newsletter: https://nicoleclarkston.com/

Facebook: https://www.facebook.com/NicoleClarkstonAuthor

Twitter: https://twitter.com/N_Clarkston

Amazon: https://www.amazon.com/Nicole-Clarkston

Austen Variations: http://austenvariations.com/

PUBLISHING

Contents

For my mother
Who knows what it's like

Foreword

The careful reader will note various references to Sir Walter Scott's writing throughout this manuscript. While it is true that Sir Walter Scott was a contemporary of Jane Austen's and much admired by her, most of his greatest works were not completed by the timeline of this tale.

I included them anyway.

Because it's fiction. I can do that.

~AJ

One

10 June 1812

D ear Darcy,

I just had word from Bowser about your fall. Bloody awful luck! Yet if my batman's intelligence is accurate and my calculations are correct, you were at least two days abed with a broken leg when you wrote your last letter and you mentioned nothing of this. The famous Darcy pride at work, I presume, but do not expect others to be so discreet about your misfortune. Half the county will have heard of it by now. I assume you have brought in none but the finest surgeon to tend your leg, but of course you will not heed his advice to keep weight off it till it is properly healed. I've no doubt you will possess a dashing limp and measure a full two inches shorter on one side by the time I return from France, but there be no man in England who could be less disadvantaged by such a handicap than yourself.

All jesting aside, I am very sorry to hear of your troubles, particularly at a time of year when you will most wish to be about the business of the estate. Pemberley's crops and lambs will thrive without your oversight, but you will be hardly fit for decent company after spending a full two months in bed. It is a pity we had sent Georgiana to Ramsgate this spring, for she could have provided some relief to your present state. Perhaps you will have to take up your quill again for some amusement while you recover. I heartily wish you a speedy and complete healing.

All is well here, if such a thing can be said of war. I've the good fortune to be stationed some miles back from the worst of the fighting, and there is word that we may be sent to Lisbon or Porto soon to aid in settling the city after the recent attacks. I confess, I would relish that assignment. They say the sun is warm and the women even warmer, so perhaps I will be able to send you a rather cheerful letter when I write again. I fear this must be short if I am to make the post, so I will detail some of the fighting for you, of the sort the broadsheets never report, in my next letter.

Do try your best to be a good patient, Darcy, for much as I have claimed to begrudge you your impressive stature, I shall not be appeased if you make yourself crooked just to suit me. Perhaps I will send a separate note to Mrs Reynolds to keep you well sedated with brandy for the next couple of months. Better yet, find something useful and challenging to pass the time, and I do not mean horseback riding.

Fondly,
Richard

Fitzwilliam Darcy to Charles Bingley

12 June 1812

D ear Bingley,
Please convey to Miss Bingley and Mrs Hurst my appreciation for their kindness. I cannot think of a more useful gift in my infirmity than a box of French fashion plates and ballroom sketches as preparation for the far-distant day when I shall presumably undertake to redecorate Pemberley. The embroidered cushion is being put to effective use, though, and Harold sends his regards.

I am more intrigued by your own news. Your father would be proud to hear you mean to purchase an estate at long last. Have you spoken to my agent? I shall post a letter to him immediately, with directions to assist you in all matters. Would that I could tour the estates with you myself! In addition to the rents and income produced by the property, be sure to inspect not only the main house but all the accessory buildings and tenant dwellings. And do not by any means fail to look over the management of the fields. It may be that you will need to make repairs to any suitable property, but it will not do to leave such intelligence until after the purchase is made.

As to my present condition, I have not left my bed in a fortnight, and I am becoming more restless than I ever was in my life. A board is strapped to either side of my right leg, and a devilish rope is looped round my ankle and secured to the foot of my bed. Carter, my family surgeon, assures me it will help the bones knit properly without bends or misalignment. I, however, am positively assured he learnt medicine at the knee of a Spanish priest. I have refused more laudanum, for its hallucinatory effects far outweigh any benefit it may have in pain relief. I have mostly been reading to distract myself, though my tastes for new books and even my old favourites have soured somewhat.

You may advise Miss Bingley that Georgiana has come away from Ramsgate earlier than expected, so any hopes of a reunion there must be deferred. The situation there was wanting, so I brought her home the very day of my accident to enjoy the rest of the summer and prepare for her expected first Season. No, she is not to come out until next year, but Lady Matlock desires to take her in hand, and I think the situation will do her much good.

Convey my felicitations to your sisters, and please assure Miss Bingley that I would be honoured to be received as a guest when you secure a property. Perhaps I will be on my feet long before you make a purchase, and I will be able to look forward to touring it with you.

Regards,
FD

Lady Catherine de Bourgh to Fitzwilliam Darcy

6 June 1812

N ephew,

I was most put out when you declined to attend me this Easter. Still, being a reasonable woman, I consoled myself with the knowledge that you would undoubtedly come in May after Georgiana had been settled in her establishment. I suppose there was nothing to be done about Fitzwilliam's assignment, but I protest your judgment that he could not have been recalled for my Eastertide service. My word commands respect from the highest quarters. No general would refuse my request if made in a timely manner, and I shall not forgive you for preventing me from writing.

However, that is nothing to this recent insult. What respectable gentleman disregards his previous engagements and throws all caution to the wind, such as you have done? A fall from your horse, indeed! I should have expected such behaviour from a callow youth, not a man of seven and twenty years! And now I suppose you will claim to be bound to your chair for some months to come. Such is the way of so-called gentlemen these days, but in my day, a man fastened a stake to his ankle, took up a cane, and kept to his duties.

I shall expect to see you at Michaelmas, if not sooner. Know that I intend to write to Fitzwilliam's regiment to have him recalled for a month's stay, for I greatly depend upon both of you. I shall not be disappointed again.

(Hereon affixed the great seal of)
Lady Catherine de Bourgh

Private Diary of Georgiana Darcy

8 June 1812

T oday I went outside.

It felt lovely, the sun on my shoulders. I told my maid I was only keeping to the portico, but the moment I was out of the house, I could not help it. I ran for the opening in the hedgerows, where I could be assured of being utterly alone. Then I peeled off my bonnet and just spread my arms and let my face shine up to the sun. For a second, I was warm everywhere, and with my eyes closed, the sky was even brighter against my skin.

And then I felt so terribly guilty that I tied my bonnet down tight and sneaked back to the house. How could I enjoy something so simple as a sunny day when Fitzwilliam is suffering so? Would that our places were reversed! I think few people would be troubled if it were me in that bed, but all the world seems to stop without Fitzwilliam to drive it forward.

He has been urging me to play my pianoforte. He even lied that he could hear me from his bedroom, and that it would cheer him as well, but I know that was just him trying to make me feel better. I should find comfort in the things that have always made me happy, he says. But he does not take that advice himself, for his books are piled unread beside his bed and his chess board sits untouched on the table.

I think he has really been more ill than he will allow. I cannot say for certain, as I have rarely been admitted to his sickroom. But surely, he would be reading voraciously if he were able, and it quite makes me afraid that he has not asked for more books. I am told he is mostly just sleeping and petting that ugly old drover dog, Harold. Harold refuses to leave his side, and Fitzwilliam has given him a fine embroidered cushion beside his own pillow. I thought the dog must be wanting some time outdoors, so I tried taking him for a walk myself, but he only sat squarely on his haunches and made me drag him up the street. I suppose he does not like London.

Neither do I. I look forward to the day when Fitzwilliam is well enough to return to Pemberley. Perhaps there, he can grow strong again and I can forget this last month, like a bad dream.

Two

12 June 1812

D ear Richard,

If our aunt carries her way, you will spend the winter in Kent rather than on the sunny shores of Portugal. I had informed her of the folly of her intent this spring, but she is not to be dissuaded by such as I. I shall let the war office disabuse her of her schemes. Better yet, perhaps I shall pray that she succeeds against all reason, and you return home sooner than hoped.

You are correct that not all is as well here as might be expected. Perhaps you did not note that my last letter came from London, not Derbyshire, so your reply was first diverted to Pemberley before finding its way here. I would have vastly preferred to cripple myself in the country, where I can at least while away my recuperative hours near a window looking out on the meadow. I suppose it is my good fortune to be in London, however, for I have had the king's own surgeon called to consult on my progress. It is slow, by the way, but I shall make a complete recovery before summer's end.

I will confess to some setbacks, but on the whole, I should declare my present trials a mere inconvenience. Indeed, my first reply to your letter was penned nearly as soon as I could sit erect, but as you guessed, I had suffered some illusion of privacy in those first few days. I see that is not to be the case, since even your batman caught some rumour all the way from London. Lord Matlock himself has waited on me in my sick room, so there is no hope of privacy. I am assured that an investigation is now being made into the maintenance of the bridle paths around Hyde Park, to prevent such a slip as my horse had from bringing down any more society bucks. We certainly cannot have the Season commence with an insufficiency of two-legged gentleman to escort this year's fresh crop of debutantes to the balls.

I would not have you fret yourself over me, however, for Georgiana and I are in constant concern for you. Are you truly safe? None can dispute your courage or your heart, but I am selfish enough to hope that no ailment or wound may touch you. I am rather fond of you, you see, and moreover, Georgiana quite depends on your safe return to us. I suppose it will do no harm to cheer on our aunt's efforts to bring you back to English shores, even if it means a month in Kent for the both of us.

FD

Doctor Elton Carter to Doctor Bernard Fitzher-
bert

13 June 1812

My dear sir,

I am honoured by your recent letter regarding Mr
Fitzwilliam Darcy, Esquire. It was a great kindness of His
Majesty to spare your services at the behest of Lord Matlock.
I am greatly in your debt for your wisdom and experience in
this case.

However, I do not believe the gentleman in question will
submit to your recommendation of amputating the injured
limb. I have been acquainted with three generations of Darcys, and the present head of the family is no less rigidly
stubborn than his grandsire, may God rest his soul. While you
and I are aware of the dangers presented by a compound-
ed, twisting fracture such as Mr Darcy sustained, he makes
light of his injuries and has adamantly refused the very same
recommendation for more than ten days now. I believe he is
perfectly convinced that he will be walking by July and riding
by September.

I appeal to your expertise. His fever is beginning to abate
somewhat, which gives me hope for the best, but all reason
and good sense advise me to remain cautious. Is there not
some further means of eliminating the risk of a blood infec-
tion? And if the gentleman should survive this most trying
period of his recovery, is there any hope that he may walk

again? My colleagues all assure me there is not, but I am hopeful that your greater knowledge might supersede theirs.

I remain yours most respectfully,
Doctor Elton Carter

Private Diary of Fitzwilliam Darcy

14 June 1812

One does not know boredom until one is forced to idleness. And one does not know sheer panic and despair until one has no control over his circumstances.

It is now sixteen days since the accident. At first was only pain—pain everywhere, for I believe I have some cracked ribs and probably a sprain to my shoulder in addition to my leg. But four days later came the fever. I fear I spent the better part of a week not in my senses. Bless Mrs Carson, for she kept Georgiana blissfully unaware of the true nature of my condition. To my knowledge, she believed I was merely sleeping each time she was turned away. But I am not ignorant of the terror in Carter's eyes each time he examines me. Perhaps he is right to fear the worst, but I am not yet prepared to confess it.

I have tried to keep alert, lest he come at me with his instruments while I am incoherent. I am still feverish, but no longer completely delirious. I think that a hopeful sign, but

Carter remains close-lipped. I believe it was three days ago I could finally sit up over ten minutes together. I have attended to my correspondence to the best of my ability, but a simple note to Bingley took me two days to compose. This entry has taken a mere hour and a quarter, which is some improvement.

What I would give for some diversion! I believe it would liven my interest enough to keep my mind alert, but none of my usual pursuits can produce even a spark of energy. I take comfort in petting Harold and trying to find a position that does not hurt my ribs.

Three

7 May 1812

D ear Sir,
   My name is Elizabeth Bennet, and I am writing to
you regarding several books my father recently rediscovered
in his collection. I believe you must have a very fine shop,
for the selections are all of the highest quality and in pristine
condition. He is greatly amused by one *Roxana*, though I am
not entirely familiar with the plot of that particular novel. I am
an admirer of Fanny Burney's books, *Evelina* and *Camilla*.

   I do hope I have found the right person to write to. There
is some doubt, you see, for the mark on the inside flap of
the books is very smudged, almost illegible. However, after

examining all of them together, taking into account their similarities, I believe I have pieced together your name and direction well enough to chance writing. We think the books had all been originally from your warehouse, and my father thinks they came into our possession when he purchased them from a gentleman in reduced circumstances, whom he met in London several years ago.

My reason for writing is this. Our village of Meryton does have a bookshop, but the proprietor is exceedingly dull in what he will order. This, combined with my father's disdain for Town and his desire that not all the neighbours should know his every book purchase, has made it difficult to add to our modest collection.

I have been saving my pin money for a long while, and I am hoping to secure something novel and unusual to surprise my father on his birthday. I believe you to have excellent taste, and if it is not too much trouble, I hope you can recommend something to a gentleman who has already read most of the popular novels. I enclose a list of the books currently in our collection, with his favourites marked, so you may have some place to begin your recommendations.

I thank you in advance for your time and consideration.

Elizabeth Bennet,
Longbourn

Mr Fitzwilliam Darcy to Miss Elizabeth Bennet

18 June 1812

D ear Miss Bennet,
	I am in receipt of your letter requesting information about your books. I see by the date that it was written several weeks past, and I can explain something of the misdirection. Mr George Darcy was my father, who passed on five years ago. My family hails from Derbyshire, but not the town of Derby. Moreover, I am presently in London, and the post took some while in finding me.

I am most intrigued by your letter. From the list you have provided, I am afraid I have regrettable news for you. The books in your collection were stolen seven years ago by one my family once trusted. I presume he is the one who took them to London or elsewhere to sell for as much as he could, and I am surprised the mark on the cover was merely smudged and not blacked out or removed entirely. I am glad to hear they found their way into the hands of one who will appreciate them. Pray, do not feel badly on account of the theft, for it certainly was none of your doing, nor should your family lose by it. The loss had already been written off and forgotten on my part.

Upon reading your list and preferred selections, I do have a recommendation for you. I see that both works of great literature and those of a lighter nature have been marked but being as this is intended as a birthday gift, I shall recommend something with both qualities. Perhaps your father will enjoy *The Adventures of Peregrine Pickle*. I assure you; the tale is as amusing as the title, and I happen to have a copy to hand. I enclose it with this letter, and in return, perhaps your father will reply with his thoughts on the book.

I am glad you thought to write to me, and I hope I have been of some service.

Fitzwilliam Darcy

Miss Elizabeth Bennet to Miss Jane Bennet

20 June 1812

M y dearest Jane,

    If you do not hasten back from London, I shall not be responsible for what Lydia means to do to your wardrobe, nor my own actions in retaliation.

I am in jest, but only half so, for today I caught our youngest sister trying on your newest bonnet, the one Mama insisted you buy before going to London. And where do you think she was when I discovered her? Why, the henhouse, of course, for she had embellished the trim somewhat with brown feathers she found in the straw. I daresay her additions did no harm to the bonnet's original aesthetics—it was very clever of you to "forget" to pack it—but she is very bold, is our young sister. Next, she will be pilfering your undergarments, for yours are the only ones long enough for her, and Mama would never know the difference.

How is Aunt recovering from her confinement? I simply cannot wait to meet our new cousin, but I fear the only thing greater than my impatience is Mama's desire to catch us both wealthy husbands. She solemnly charged me to remind you of your "duty" while in town, but she seems to think no London gentleman could possibly be interested in me. Therefore, she keeps inviting John Lucas and Marcus Danforth and Elliot Goulding to dinner. Never mind that John Lucas has scarcely enough inheritance to even call himself a gentleman, and Elliot Goulding has crested the hill of middle age and is firmly commencing his descent down the back side. Marcus Danforth is almost a decentish sort of fellow, if he did not insist on licking the food from his teeth every time he passes the mirror in the hall. Mary says it is not Christian to mimic him, as if trying to retrieve parsley from my own teeth, thus causing him to keep rubbing at his gums when he thinks no one is looking.

Jane, I have a curious bit of news. Do you recall that book Papa always chuckled over and would never let us read? He still will not surrender it to me, which leads me to think its content might be indecent. However, I glimpsed the inside cover some while back, and it bore a magnificent crest—or what was left of one. Papa has grudgingly permitted me to organize his bookshelves, and I found at least twenty novels shoved behind others or tucked under his estate books. Among them, I discovered almost a dozen more books with the same mark as the one he likes so well. Two of them have become my personal favourites.

When I asked Papa about the mark, he said he was in London once, waiting for Mama outside a milliner's shop, when he met a very smart-looking young gentleman wearing a mourning cloth. The man was pockets to let and was sadly selling all his books. Papa said he asked about the mark and the young man said that his books were a gift from his father, and originally came from a very fine shop in Derby that sold books at wholesale. Papa felt sorry for him and bought the entire collection, though did not trouble himself to learn any more because he got the books so cheaply. Well, I was not sure where to start, and Uncle could provide very little help, so I sent off an arrow into the darkness, as it were. I wrote to the shop to see if they had more of the same. It was just after you left for London, so it had been many weeks and I had despaired of an answer.

But two days ago, I had a reply. Not just a reply, for the shop owner sent a gift! He certainly did not need to, as we learned the books had actually been stolen and the young "mourner" my father met was probably the thief. I shall have to repay his kindness, for indeed no book seller can remain in business by giving away his books or letting them be stolen without seeking reparations. I mean to buy as many as I can afford, and I thought I would ask you if you had any requests. Perhaps Aunt would like a book on nursery rhymes? Better yet, our uncle might consider trading with him. It sounds as though the man is even in London for some while, by the direction he sent in his letter.

Mrs Hill just brought me some tea, and she says to remind you to ask Aunt's cook for the lemon biscuit receipt. I am taking tea in my room this afternoon because Mary is determinedly banging away at some concerto she is trying to perfect. I think she fancies Marcus Danforth, who is to come to dinner tonight.

Pray for me, lest I lose my eternal soul over a parsley leaf.
Lizzy

Four

Lord Matlock to John Talbot, Steward of Pemberley

19 June 1812

M r Talbot,

I have just come from the bedside of your master, my nephew, Mr Fitzwilliam Darcy. I freely acknowledge that I write out of my own compunction, and without Darcy's knowledge.

I feel you ought to be prepared for any and all outcomes concerning your master. One moment he looks at Death's door with fever, and the next he rallies himself to apparent wellness out of sheer obstinacy. The surgeon is quite guarded when we speak, but one thing he has told me is that he has never seen such a break as Darcy's where the patient recovered... and kept the limb, that is.

Darcy is taking up his pen, but I daresay he is too unwell to have the sense to direct you in certain matters, and no doubt too stubborn to admit to their necessity. However, I recommend you put affairs in order so a proper accounting of all Pemberley's assets and obligations can be rendered at any moment it is desired. I shall direct my steward at Matlock, Purvis, to be at your disposal should any assistance be required.

You may reach me in London for the present. I will keep you apprised of circumstances as it seems right.

Ralph Fitzhugh, Lord Matlock

Fitzwilliam Darcy to Lord Walton

19 June 1812

M y lord,

I have not slighted your daughter on purpose. Indeed, I was eagerly anticipating dining with your family on the twenty-second, but I have been unable to leave my immediate quarters for three weeks. I regret that my man of business somehow neglected to inform you of my mishap until two days prior to the occasion, but I was likewise unaware that the purpose of the evening was so that I might wait on Miss

Emmeline. Had I been informed thus in the original invitation, I surely would have taken care not to break my leg until after the dinner party.

I remain yours respectfully,
Fitzwilliam Darcy

Miss Caroline Bingley to Miss Georgiana Darcy

25 June 1812

M y dearest Georgiana,

How we all long for your company! My brother, as you know, has finally brought us to Ramsgate for the sea bathing. I confess, darling, I had not expected it to be so bracing, as the weather is unseasonably warm even for this time of year. But how wrong I was! Why, my teeth chattered to great effect, and I am quite sure my blood has been invigorated by the experience. They say it is the finest thing there is for a lady's constitution, and my dear, you know how ladies must possess an air of health and vitality.

I found the dearest little necklace yesterday in one of the shops, and I was telling Louisa how very much it reminded me of that quaint little bauble I recall you wearing when you were but a girl. I declare, it put me so much in mind of you that I nearly purchased it just to keep in my own collection to pass on to another little girl someday. But there, as Louisa recalled to me, there is no purpose in a lady spending her scant pin money on such frivolities. Let her husband bear the expense of necklaces for little girls, should there be any—of course, after the lady provides her husband with an heir.

Are you certain you cannot be prevailed upon to join us before the summer is out? It shall be ever so dull without you. Why, even the salons and the dinner parties hold little appeal for me without my particular young friend near, as I had so dearly hoped. We shall stay another month complete, at the very least. The Hursts have determined to remain here while Charles begins his search for suitable estates. He has gone to Cambridge to learn about some little place, though I am sure it cannot suit from what he tells me. Only twenty bedrooms, can you imagine? For my part, I should like to be settled farther north, and I have informed my brother so.

I do dearly hope your own brother is faring well. We hear so little of him, with Charles gone to the north. I imagine he is rallying all his strength to be recovered for the shooting this autumn, as I know the gentleman are all so fond of doing. Surely, we will be settled in an estate of our own before then, but if not, I am certain they will all wish to come to Pemberley as they have done every year. And of course, what is a day spent shooting birds if a gentleman cannot enjoy fair companionship by evening? I daresay, my darling, after your come-out we will have such balls and soirees as Derbyshire has not seen in a generation.

I am most affectionately yours,
Caroline Bingley

Fitzwilliam Darcy to John Talbot

30 June 1812

T albot,
     No, it is not necessary for you to gather the estate books as though I were on my deathbed. I assure you, that is far from the case. Lord Matlock is to be commended for his foresight in matters of business, but I am not his business. Please carry on as you were and do not feel obliged to report your doings to Purvis at Matlock.

The Suffolks are growing well according to your recent report. The shorthorns concern me, though. Your weight estimates show them far under what they should be at this time of year. Have you no explanation for the stillbirths we saw earlier this season? Perhaps there is something amiss in the meadows. Have Jeffers conduct another thorough inspection to search for noxious weeds, and do not neglect to look for evidence of predators near the grazing areas.

You may tell Mrs Reynolds to put aside Miss Darcy's letter requesting that her rooms be prepared for her. I have spoken to her on the matter, and she will remain in London with me for the present. I am sorry that the new pianoforte is to be delivered in our absence, but I have ordered a second for the townhouse to appease Miss Darcy until late summer, when I anticipate being able to make the journey north.

Regarding Mr Smithers being kicked by his mule; see to it that the kitchen provides a basket each Sunday for his wife. His arm should mend long before harvest time, but inquire of Mr Michaels to see if he can spare any of his help for a month or two, at my expense. I should not like for Mr Smithers to find himself in any straits before winter that can be averted by the aid of his neighbours.

Please send me your figures again at the end of the month.

Sincerely,
Fitzwilliam Darcy

Five

Mr Thomas Bennet to Mr Fitzwilliam Darcy

2 July 1812

D ear Mr Darcy,

I have rarely been so delighted as I was with the gift my daughter presented me for my birthday this year. My Elizabeth knows her old father's heart, to be sure, and I was greatly amused to hear how she found you out at last. I confess to far too little curiosity about that collection of books I purchased several years ago. I was only pleased to find such quality for such a low price, and I still struggle to remember the particulars of the transaction. No doubt, Mrs Bennet had dragged me to Town on some mission to unburden all London of its lace, and I was biding my time waiting for her to purchase the rest of the warehouse.

It does trouble me to learn that the books were stolen. I am aware of the true worth of such books, and I enclose a draft on my bank to help defray the loss to you. I am afraid a full repayment of the value of the books must wait till after this year's harvest, so I shall promise to send you the rest, and as the kind soul my daughter believes you to be, you will assure me that is not necessary, and we shall both be content. I do relish the notion of a correspondent with whom to discuss my favourite books. Tell me, what are your thoughts on Sir Walter Scott? Do you believe his works will stand the test of a generation, or is he merely the delight of the moment?

Elizabeth has asked to include her own note of gratitude with mine. Of all my daughters, she is the least silly, and the most likely to appreciate a good novel. I will add that her penmanship is excelled only by my Jane's, so you should find it quite legible—although, I suppose you know that already. No doubt she will scarcely be able to contain her desire to order more books, but I beg of you, have mercy on my purse. Lord knows I would sneak a bit more into her reticule just for the pleasure of seeing which books she would choose, but Mrs Bennet is placing heavy demands on me this year with a fifth daughter now out in company and needing gowns.

I look forward to hearing from you if you so desire.
Thomas A. Bennet

Miss Elizabeth Bennet to Mr Fitzwilliam Darcy

2 July 1812

D ear Sir,

   I desired to write sooner to you with my gratitude, but my next younger sister, Mary, threatened a fit of pious apoplexy when I spoke of it. For all I know, according to her, you could be a single gentleman and my reputation would now be in tatters! I have reminded her that when she sends away for her piano music, she is probably corresponding with someone of the opposite sex, but she declares that since she does not know their name, it must be all right.

   I had the pleasure of reading *Peregrine Pickle* before I wrapped it to give to my father. Ah, yes, it was terrible of me, but I am a fast reader and I do not think I left too many crumbs between the pages. There I am in jest, because only the most despicable person could defile a book so, and I do not think I am very despicable. I imagine the real shock and scandal would be in that I read the book at all, for our hero became rather dissolute in parts of his life, did he not? My father should roundly chastise me for reading his gift before I gave it to him, shouldn't he? I suppose I shall have to ask him to correct me through some penance.

   I must say, I thought the book quite instructive in some facets. Is it intended to be so? I found the descriptions of young Peregrine's indifferent parents rather unsettling, and I cannot quite put my finger on the reason for it. On the whole, however, I greatly enjoyed his irreverence for the holy grails of society. Nothing was quite so sacred that our dear author could not twist it to examine its follies, much to the reader's amusement. And now you must be thinking what a shocking lady I am. I assure you; you do not know the half of it, for after I finish this letter, I mean to take a jaunt through the woods in nothing but my morning dress and house slippers. Mama despairs of me.

I hope I have written tartly enough to impress you with my sincerity, for I am deeply appreciative of your kindness in sending such a gift. As you did not ask for payment, I shall instead order a second book, and I enclose what I hope is enough to pay twice the price. Pray, surprise me with your selection, for I quite like your taste.

Yours in bookish camaraderie,
Elizabeth Bennet

Mr Fitzwilliam Darcy to Mr Thomas Bennet

4 July 1812

Dear Mr Bennet,

I fear you and your good daughter must be labouring under a false impression, and it is to my regret that I did not correct it sooner. I am not, nor have I ever been, a purveyor of fine books. I am, rather, a private gentleman who, like yourself, finds delight in a profound thought and a well-turned phrase.

Upon re-reading my initial letter from Miss Elizabeth Bennet, I understand her assumptions a little more clearly than at my first reading. I have been recovering from a rather inconvenient accident which rendered me temporarily discomposed, and I am mortified to discover how little the circumstances of the first letter impressed me at the time. I will confess myself quite charmed by the tone of the letter, and being frightfully bored and in need of some diversion, I was pleased to be of some service. Were it not that disguise is my abhorrence, I suspect I might have been content to perpetuate the misconception, for I was more amused by your recent letters than by anything else this past month.

I return to you your cheque, for though it was a laudable notion to repay me, it is unnecessary. I also return Miss Bennet's money, but with a caveat. I ask that one or both of you should read this second book I enclose, and then respond with your thoughts when you return it to me. I quite look forward to your reply.

Sincerely,
Fitzwilliam Darcy

Six

6 July 1812

M y dearest cousin Richard,

Your letter was ever so cheerful. Are you really being sent to Lisbon? Oh, you must tell me all about it! I know very little of the place, but it sounds so very exotic. Is it quite warm? Are there truly pirates to be found in port? I suppose I shall have to wait for all those answers until you receive this.

You asked about Fitzwilliam, and I do not quite know how to reply. I am not privy to all you wished to know, but I think it is true that he was terribly feverish for many days. How many I do not know, for they all seemed to blend together, and no one tells me anything. I think he is somewhat better now. At least, he is sitting up for longer spells and Doctor Carter seems less grave. I think it is still very bad, though.

I overheard the doctor muttering something to another doctor he had brought with him, and they seem to think Fitzwilliam's leg may never set properly. It is because it twisted so when he fell, you see. It was not merely the bone but the sinews, which they say may take months longer to mend than the bone itself. They say his foot had been caught in the irons, and his horse dragged him some distance. Did he not tell you how bruised he was when we brought him home? I think he has been very sly with you, Richard, but I am certain it is only because he did not wish to worry you.

As for me, I am well enough. Ramsgate was not half so charming as I had hoped. The place itself was delightful in every way, but I seem to have been greatly deceived in the company. As I think back on the three weeks I spent there thinking myself quite happy, the shine of the memory has tarnished somewhat. No, that is not quite right. Even sweet memories have turned bitter, and I cannot but think on them with abhorrence. There, that is a word Fitzwilliam uses all the time, and I shall endeavour to use it more, for any resemblance that is more like my brother and less like my naïve self cannot serve me ill.

I write in riddles, and I know it is cruel of me, but my brother says I should write nothing that would worry you. And so, let us speak only of pleasant things, for I dearly love hearing from you.

Fitzwilliam just called me above stairs to ask how I like my new piano, for he has not seen it yet. It is exquisite, but I can hardly bring myself to play until he can hear it. I offered instead to take that awful Harold for a walk, but the little brute tried to bite me. He has become ever so protective!

I think I will apply myself to my playing this evening and think fondly on you, my favourite cousin. If only Cousin Sophia and Cousin Anne were so easy to confide in!

Yours,
Georgiana

Mrs Madeline Gardiner to Miss Elizabeth Bennet

10 July 1812

M y dear Lizzy,
There truly is nothing sweeter in this world than
baby Elinor's darling little hand nestled in my shawl as she
sleeps, unless it is the dimple in her soft cheek. Oh, how I
long for you to see her! One would think after four babies I
would be less enraptured by their novelty, but I think I am
more smitten with her than I ever was with Edmund or Daniel
or even my sweet Rose. Your uncle swears he does not see
it, but I fancy Elinor already has the Gardiner nose, and her
eyes favour your grandmother—or rather you, since you are
the only other in the family to inherit them.

You are very kind to ask after my health, but I assure you,
I am perfectly well, just as I was the last time I wrote. My
dear Lizzy, I really thought you more sly than that! Your real
purpose in asking after me is to learn whether I am receiving
callers, and, of course, to find out how Jane has been occupy-
ing herself. She is too modest to say, and there may be nothing
in it, but your uncle tells me that a certain Mr Mayberry,

nephew of my good friend Mrs Watson, has called twice now "with his aunt's compliments." There, make of that what you will.

I am astonished to hear that you at last solved the riddle of the books! And it was not a shop in Derby, but a private gentleman? How very curious! Indeed, it was probably prudent of you not to write his name, for you cannot be too careful with your reputation. Your bookish correspondent may feel the same. Best not to put it out that you have been writing to someone who might be known, even if it is something so innocent. But you must promise to give me the occasional hint, should you and your father keep up the acquaintance. Remember that I am from Derbyshire myself, so who knows but that I may be able to guess his name?

Your uncle has been working exceeding long days of late. He is taking on a new assistant and though it ought to permit him more liberty by autumn, he is kept very busy just now. I am not insensitive to your hope of taking some holiday with us, but with baby Elinor still so small and the warehouse as it is, perhaps we must wait until next summer. I would dearly love to show you the Lake country.

Edmund and Daniel have just returned from their airing with Jane, and I promised to take tea with them. Do not neglect to write more of your mystery friend!

Aunt Madeline

Seven

11 July 1812

Y ou may well be surprised to see my handwriting on the note, even though my father is the one who wrapped this book for the post. He will have read this beforehand and presumably approved of its content.

I have long been familiar with Samuel Johnson's writing, but *Rasselas* was a revelation. Before I take the trouble of setting down my thoughts, I shall sit and ponder a moment what yours may be. I know little of you, save that you must have to hand a great many books and that you write with a bit of irony dripping from your pen. This cements you as one of my favourite people without ever having met you. You seem to me a man who lives within the pages of the book, rather than merely admiring it for a fine cover or a fashionable inscription. Therefore, there must be some reason you chose this particular book to send, and not merely because it was convenient.

And now, I shall engage in a cheeky flight of fancy. This Rasselas, being the prince of Abyssinia, was shut up in a valley of pleasures, where he might have everything his heart desired but freedom. He was a bit like a fattened goose, was he not, kept happy until the whims of others should decide upon another fate for him. Except that he was not happy, was he? For he dreamt of nothing but escape. Yet, when this escape was effected, he did not find what he sought. It was quite a gloomy book, and complete happiness was always just out of reach for our hero.

And now, sir, I shall probably offend you greatly. You have said that some misfortune befell you, and you are presently indisposed. Are you, like our prince, languishing in an opulent prison, without joy or prospect of freedom? Surely, I am merely suffering from an overactive imagination. But one does wonder these things.

We thank you most earnestly for the loan of this splendid book. And if I have not presumed too much, please write again and tell me if I was at all correct. If so, I shall take care to send you a great many impertinent letters guaranteed to either make you smile or give you an object to be truly offended over.

Elizabeth Bennet

Mr Fitzwilliam Darcy to Miss Elizabeth Bennet

13 July 1812

D ear Miss Bennet,

I believe you must be an enchantress of some kind. I'd no notion that merely loaning a book to a stranger could grant them such clear insight into my soul! You have put into a handful of words something I had struggled to describe, even to myself.

Indeed, I am housed in comfort, and I thank my father and his progenitors for the good fortunes bestowed upon me in that regard. But I am presently trapped by a broken frame and tormented by my inability to right certain wrongs. I am no fit company for those dear to me, and I have been set at odds against even those who laboured to save my very life at the onset of my trial. It would not be fitting to describe more of that trouble to a lady. I shall only say that I look about me and see few I can trust, even when everyone about is employed to my benefit in some way or another.

So, yes, please send your impertinent letters. I would not wish to risk your reputation (or my own, for that matter), so if it be troublesome to keep your correspondence discreet, I perfectly understand. But you did succeed in making me smile rather than offending me.

In anticipation of your next impertinence,
Fitzwilliam Darcy

Mr Charles Bingley to Mr Fitzwilliam Darcy

29 July 1812

D ear Darcy,

I was pleased to see you when I came to Town last week. I feared your doctor would have barred the door. I had a word with Miss Georgiana after I saw you, and I hope I was able to cheer her. She looks rather melancholy, Darcy. I assume it is only fear for you, but I have never seen her so downcast. I hope you have recovered your strength some more since I saw you.

You asked me to keep you advised of my search, so I write to do so. My solicitor has heard of a property in Hertfordshire that is not for sale, but to let. From what he writes of the property, it sounds as if it would suit perfectly, but I had taken the notion of purchasing. What do you think? Is it a waste of time and effort to take a property only temporarily? Or ought I to count it as valuable experience in managing an estate, while I continue my search for something else?

I have attached his estimates of the rents and the value of the property. Truly, it sounds as if it might be just the thing. I would have preferred to secure something closer to Pemberley, but this is an easy distance from London, so the location has its charms.

Pray, take care to heed your doctor's instructions. I am certain he is right that you must keep the room dark and restful, and that all the windows ought to be closed against a draft. I know it is rather suffocating in the summer, but I am sure he knows what is best. All will be well soon!

Sincerely,

CB

Colonel Richard Fitzwilliam to Lord Matlock

2 August 1812

D ear Father,

I am glad to hear that your gout has troubled you less this summer. It is indeed a relief, particularly with our Sophia preparing for her second Season. All those endless balls on your feet will be less odious. Has Sophia many suitors in Town? I recall how she used to say no one would pay court to her unless I was stationed on the Continent; too far away to harass any young bucks who would dare to speak to my sister. I am sure she was in jest, but I should hope my absence has been fruitful in some way or another.

I am well, and quite safe where I am. The Camp Disease had me low for some while, but thanks to Bowser's care, I am fully recovered. The general keeps me close to his tent, and I have been able to secure what comforts are available for my men. We have lost very few men and horses to injury or illness, and spirits are high, despite the heat of summer. It is certain now that we will be sent to Portugal, so you may tell Mother that I couldn't be safer in her own drawing room than I shall be this autumn.

Is Darcy really so incapacitated as you and Georgiana say? His letters gave no indication of it. He did confess to being abed with a broken leg, but according to your last letter, he was tottering on the brink of death for many weeks. Odd, how a man who could probably unhorse my best cavalry fighters could take an innocent tumble in Hyde Park and nearly lose his life for it. Fortune is strange!

If it is not too much trouble, will you ask Mother to look in on Georgiana from time to time? I imagine she must be feeling gloomy with Darcy injured. I do not know why he would not have left her in Ramsgate for the summer. The situation was everything delightful for a girl of sixteen, and I think she would have grown much from the experience. Certainly, she would have been happier there than haunting the halls of Darcy House all summer.

I would write more, but there is a shortage of paper in camp at present, and I never was good at crossing my lines neatly enough for it to be read. Kiss Sophia for me and give Mother my regards.

Richard

Eight

3 August 1812

I t is now more than two months since The Incident that has altered the course of my life. I am frankly horrified at how little progress has been made toward healing. My leg still looks like something from the butcher's window, and every movement still engenders such popping and shifting of my bones and ligaments that I can scarcely help crying out.

Carter swears it is because I do not lie quietly in my bed and I keep ordering the windows to be opened, letting in diseased air. But I will not swelter in the darkness, and how can the air from the London streets be any worse than the air I have already expelled from my lungs? So, yes, the windows are open, and the drapes drawn.

I have never felt so helpless in my life, nor so little inclined to do something about it. I am not at ease asking Georgiana to sit with me, though she does every morning. She ought not to be staring at my bed, bound to the same prison as I. I would have her out playing her piano or walking the small flower garden, but she has not rallied herself to do it. I wish she would forget what happened and cease blaming herself. Indeed, she erred, but I do not hold her at fault. Much as she claims to want to bring me cheer, I do not see how she can find joy herself if she insists on sitting by my side. I must stay here, but she need not.

Richard writes to me once every week, and Bingley twice. I could have done little for Richard, but for Bingley, I would have wished to attend him as he takes these critical steps toward his future. Perhaps it is well that I am not there, for he is sounding more assured of himself with every decision he is forced to make without me. Yet, if I know Bingley, he will settle on some new estate and marry the closest neighbour with blue eyes and too wide of a smile. That is his sort of woman, and I can only pray that when he finds her, she is worthy of his gentle character. Let him not fall to a mercenary family, I pray!

I am afraid I may have fallen myself, though. My only delight is when the post arrives from Miss Elizabeth Bennet. She has written a dozen letters to me by now, each more irreverent than the last. How could a woman I have never met, whose manner of expression could only be described as forward and inquisitive, have made such inroads into my heart? How could she, whose face I have never seen, see me so clearly? No, I am not in love with a woman I do not know, but I am in love with her letters.

How my father would scold me! And I wonder at her father for permitting her to write, but I selfishly hope he does nothing to check her. He writes short notes himself, with about every third or fourth letter from her, and he always seals and sends the post under his name. He sounds a sardonic and perhaps a dilatory fellow who finds more enjoyment in reading his daughter's words than penning his own. He usually speaks of chess or books or how much his wife is demanding for new gowns for their daughters. There are five of them! I pity the man nearly as much as he pities himself. Diverting, practical and piquant, his letters are well worth the read.

But Miss Elizabeth's letters are worth committing to memory, and I have done so. I wonder how old she is, and what she looks like. I am not indifferent to her station in life, which must be beneath my own, but she has something I do not. She has joy, and with each letter I receive from her, a bit of it sheds from the pages into my fingers. She can tease without belittling and call me to frankness without offending.

She is probably a mere child, or betrothed elsewhere, or perhaps even a spinster double my age. Such is my luck. But I have spent many an idle hour wondering about her. I keep selecting books to send her based on what I would like to learn of her in her replies. Today, I sent her a volume of Sir Walter Scott's poems.

Perhaps, one day when I have recovered my strength and my dignity sufficiently, I may seek a way to meet her. But at present, I desire no one to see me but Harold.

Miss Elizabeth Bennet to Miss Jane Bennet

6 August 1812

M y darling Jane,

      Cover your ears and close the shutters. Draw the drapes and speak only in whispers, and do not by any means cry out in alarm, lest Mama overhear you all the way from Town.

I am in love.

See, I knew you would leap to that conclusion. Stop it at once, for I do not speak of any mortal man. Not even an angel! Lean close to the page and promise me you will burn this letter once it is read. Are you quite ready to learn how I met my prince?

I was out walking this morning, and there was a grain sack wiggling in the ditch. What do you think? Some brute had cast off the dearest, ugliest little mongrel puppy ever to wallow in the mud! Naturally, I brought him home, over Papa's protests, I might add. He is presently curled in my lap, trying to eat my fingers off. He ruined my frock earlier, and he has already chewed up that former bonnet of yours that Lydia so carelessly left out. That alone ought to endear him to you.

Mama has not ceased lamenting my hoydenish ways, bringing home a mutt someone else tried to dispose of. No doubt he is riddled with vermin, but he can be bathed. He has better manners than Marcus Danforth, and his breath is sweeter than Elliot Goulding's. I have decided to name him Prince George, but do not ask me the reason. I am not certain myself. Mary thinks it proof that I am hopelessly irreverent, but I could have told her that long ago.

Is our little Cousin Elinor growing more beautiful each day? Of course, she is. And has... ahem... our aunt received any callers with handsome sons or nephews to dispose of? You must tell me every detail, so I may try to decide if any hopeful gentleman is worthy of you. I shall charge Uncle most seriously with the duty of running off any man who is not.

How is my own quest for love proceeding? Not well, unless you count Prince George or my Gentleman of the Books. As one is a canine and the other may well be a geriatric eccentric, for all I truly know of him, I should say my progress toward securing a good match is abysmal. But they both make me laugh, and I dearly love to laugh. As Mama says, laughter will not keep me out of the hedgerows, but I do not mean to settle for one of the three prospects she has put in my way. So, it is up to you to marry well, and I will do my best to corrupt all ten of your children.

Prince George just demonstrated to me that I have been remiss in taking him for his afternoon walk, so I had better close now. I am sure Mama's note will catch you up on all the local gossip, and Mary's will be instructive on all matters moral. Lydia and Kitty have flitted off to Meryton, so you shan't hear from them this time, and Papa may or may not add his own words to you. But we do all miss you terribly, and myself most of all.

Anxiously awaiting your return

E

Nine

Lady Catherine de Bourgh to Mr Fitzwilliam Darcy

15 August 1812

Darcy,

I grow weary of your excuses. Surely, you are well by this time. Where is your manhood? In my day, a man would exert his willpower a little and stand on two feet within a fortnight.

But there, I hear everyone has fallen after the fashion of this Beau Brummell sluggard who polishes his boots with champagne and spends most of his day at his toilette. Or are you gone to slovenly habits and neglecting to make yourself presentable at all? I suppose you have even taken to wearing trousers in the drawing room!

It is not decent, Darcy. A man must face his responsibilities. Anne has had no more than a dutiful letter from you, such as one would send to a distant relation, and not what a gentleman ought to write to his betrothed.

And how does Georgiana fare, I ask you? Lady Matlock writes she has come back to London all this summer and has not been in Ramsgate as planned. She ought to have at least come here, and not stayed alone in London with only an invalid brother to speak to.

I expect the honour of a reply by week's end. Let us set the date for your marriage and have done with it.

(Hereon affixed the great seal of)
Lady Catherine de Bourgh

Mr Fitzwilliam Darcy to the Earl of Matlock

20 August 1812

U ncle,
        I freely acknowledge that I must be indebted to you for your pains on my behalf. However, I do not believe it necessary to ask your solicitor to oversee my steward's management of Pemberley's accounts. John Talbot is honest and competent, and his task is not lightened by asking him to report to another. I am perfectly lucid and capable of attending to my correspondence.

I deeply appreciate your desire to be of some material assistance. I would not have it said that I am ungrateful, but I no longer have one foot in the grave. Pray, if it be on your conscience to lend me aid of some sort, perhaps you would have a word with Lady Catherine and Lord Walton. Both have been expressing impatience that I have not declared myself to their daughters. I should rather be able to walk before I contemplate matrimony.

Please give Lady Matlock and Lady Sophia my regards. I hope we shall all be able to be in company again soon.

Sincerely,
Fitzwilliam Darcy

Miss Elizabeth Bennet to Miss Charlotte Lucas

18 August 1812

C harlotte,

I am quite put out that the days are already growing shorter. A week ago, it was still light past eight in the evening, and now I see fingers of darkness working their way over the horizon. I say, who permitted this? I had not yet had my fill of summer sunshine and wildflowers in the meadow and fresh sweet air blowing through my bedroom by night.

Do not let it be known that I keep my windows open in the summer. I can only manage it when Jane is not there, and

Mama knows nothing of it. She is still convinced that wood nymphs will come to snatch me away under cover of darkness.

To answer your note, yes, I can come help you tie up herbs tomorrow. We shall be entirely merry and far too silly for our ages. I am glad you asked because I am greatly in need of a breather from reading. I have had my nose so deeply buried in a book of poetry today that I cannot even remember when I last ate. Oh, but it is *such* a book! I shall tell you of it tomorrow, but someone very kind lent me a copy of Sir Walter Scott's poems. Papa has been anxiously waiting for me to finish, so he may read it next, but I think I will keep it under my pillow tonight. Perhaps someday I will tell you about the friend who lent me this marvellous book.

I will see you at half-past one if that will suit. I hope I may bring Prince George, because he is very naughty when I leave him behind.

E

Private Diary of Georgiana Darcy

20 August 1812

Fitzwilliam's leg is no longer being pulled and stretched by those wretched ropes. I cannot think what a relief that must be to him! He tried to hide how great his discomfort was, but it was impossible to conceal. At least now he can turn about more in his bed. Surely, Doctor Carter was being a bit too cautious in keeping him tied up for so long, but he said he was acting under the advice of the king's own surgeon, and he must be right. But poor Fitzwilliam!

He has ordered a special chair to be made for him with wheels and a long plank stretching forward where his leg may rest. Oh, I do hope it helps! If he would only leave that miserable room now and again, I am sure he would begin to feel better. Fitzwilliam has always so longed to be useful. I have never known a time when he was not working until now.

At least he is reading books again, and he tends to the post most faithfully. That is encouraging. If Fitzwilliam can slowly resume something of his normal self, perhaps there is yet hope for me.

Ten

21 August 1812

I write to apprise you of my impressions of Sir Walter Scott, as that was what you demanded in payment for the reading of this splendid book. I hereby render unto Caesar, et cetera. Firstly, I believe a book too poor a medium to capture the qualities of his work.

What I mean by that is that on the page, the poems fall somewhat flat. But read aloud, as I read them with my father, with expression and vigour and some little dramatic flair, they come alive. I confess, I am not typically a student of verse, but I was impressed with the cadence by which he wrote. It was as if he had a metronome on his writing desk, and a music master with a conductor's stick.

Alas, that is where my compliments must end.

I hate terribly to give you pain, but I am nothing if not brutally honest. Mama says that is why I shall never catch a husband, but I should think it a sorry lot for any man to be swindled into the marital estate by a silver-tongued female. But I was speaking of Sir Walter Scott.

I think it wildly unfair that the man should endeavour to stir the heart and enrapture the mind by means of such sorcery as he possesses. It is surely beyond the talents of any mortal, and therefore, I must conclude that he must employ some manner of dark art. Take, for example, this line from *The Truth of Woman*:

> *Stamp them on the running stream, Print them on the moon's pale beam, And each evanescent letter Shall be clearer, firmer, better, And more permanent, I ween, Than the thing those letters mean.*

I ask you. Can there be found a more elegant slight of all my sex than this? In a handful of words, he claims a woman's faith is worth less than a shaft of moonlight, and yet he threads his words so brave and artful that even I can do little but swoon in awe of his pen.

And in another place, he writes an ode to, of all things, a lock of hair. Indeed, a romantic gift from fair lady, but this talisman is like to a crucifix in this poor wretch's hateful, empty existence. How, indeed, can such a soul-wrenching effluence be attributed to such an innocent item? Sorcery, I say!

There, you have my full and unredeemable opinion of Sir Walter Scott and his diabolically magnificent collection of wizardry. If you remain unconvinced that there must be something more than the natural at work amid those fair pages, I simply point you to *My Native Land*. Perhaps a man might find his "brest" rent appropriately, and then wonder at the strange power of such spare words to ravage the heart.

So, I cannot approve of his writing, for he wields some unfair advantage over others who would dare attempt to emulate him. I shall revisit this collection regularly, no doubt, just to assure myself that my opinion against him is fixed.

I sincerely hope you have no further such books. If so, you should unburden yourself of them straightaway.

Yours in concern,
Elizabeth Bennet

Mr Fitzwilliam Darcy to Miss Elizabeth Bennet

24 August 1812

Fear not, Miss Bennet, for you have successfully cautioned me against making any further attempt at reading Sir Walter Scott. So convinced am I that he must not be trusted to live longer in my library that I have made an exhaustive search among my shelves for anything that might be connected with him. You will be pleased to discover that I have enclosed them in a crate and sent them off on a pony cart to one who might be trusted with their disposition. Heaven knows we cannot risk corrupting anyone else. See that you don a blindfold and preferably gloves when you attend to the duty I ask of you.

You may now think me a terrible boor, for I shall ask one more favour. As I have fairly emptied the shelves in my private quarters, I am greatly in need of some amusement. I noted in your original list of favourite novels *The History of Charles Grandison*. I read it as a youth and am in mind to read it again.

I may certainly purchase my own copy, but I would much rather borrow yours, if I may be so bold. Even better if it has been creased and marked up, with slips of paper hid between the pages with your characteristically biting remarks. I should be curious to know how poor Charles Grandison withstood your inspection.

It is certainly your right to refuse, for I quite understand the complication of books being owned by a father or an estate, and therefore unavailable for lending. If you should find it possible, I shall recommend myself by such means as I may.

I am not insensitive to the burden of trust, depending upon another to keep his promise. Alas, I have been both victim and offender in such an arrangement, though never with malice aforethought. I am therefore all the more eager to never disappoint another person if it be in my power to avoid doing so. I view the trust of others as nearly a sacrament. I shall not break my oath to return your book promptly, and if no objection is made, accompanied by a few notes of my own, detailed specifically for your entertainment.

If I may be suffered to add one more detail to my request, I shall. I am recovering from an unfortunate incident which, by rights, ought to have killed me. I count myself blessed for my continued existence on this sphere, but my recovery is far from complete. I am shameless, you see, for your comments amuse me, and I have precious little amusement offered in the dull drear of my chamber. I pray you take pity on another poor soul, and do not accuse me of any dark arts of my own.

Yours in pernicious boredom,
Fitzwilliam Darcy

Eleven

Miss Caroline Bingley to Miss Georgiana Darcy

25 August 1812

M y dearest friend,

I have splendid news! My brother has at last settled on an estate. I regret to say it is not near Pemberley, and I confess I wept for two nights together when I learnt of it. However, I am determined to make the best of it. After all, is not Hertfordshire but half a day's drive from London? I believe I could content myself with entertaining at our country house one day and attending a ball in London the next.

My brother is furiously making his preparations to take up residence. I believe we are to arrive before Michaelmas, but I had hoped to defer him till January. The society in the country is always somewhat lacking unless one contrives to supply his own company. I am quite sure that if you and your excellent brother could find it possible to journey to us, then Louisa and I could be easily content wherever Charles determines to uproot us next.

Oh, I do hope you may join us. Think how peaceful and charming we shall all be? For I do dearly love an autumn stroll. I shall send orders to my seamstress for a few new walking gowns suitable to the season and have them waiting for me when we arrive next month.

Louisa sends her regards, and I am quite certain Charles does as well, though he would consider it ungentlemanly to ask me to put it down in my note to you. We were always so fond of you, and I dearly hope to see more of you this autumn.

Yours in felicity,
Caroline Bingley

Colonel Fitzwilliam to Mr Fitzwilliam Darcy

27 August 1812

B om dia from sunny Portugal!
We are now settled in our camp, and I have much to say about the beauty of this country. Perhaps I ought to defer my raptures for another time, however, for I am wanted in the general's tent in half an hour. I plan to send this note with

his official correspondence so that it may reach you all the sooner.

Georgiana's last letter came yesterday, just after we settled the remounts, and I confess to some concern over her tone. Our dear girl is suffering some deep regrets, is she not? But she will not say why, for fear of worrying her old cousin. I say, it has had somewhat the reverse effect. Darcy, what happened? And why does she sound as if she bears the guilt of your present troubles? I pray, answer me frankly, for if you do not, I shall hold you accountable for the charges of desertion that shall certainly follow me back home when I come to wring the answer from you in person.

There, I have delivered my threats and I have a full ten minutes before I must make myself presentable for the general. All is well here. We do not expect to see any fighting, which you may convey to my mother. The city has been left an unholy mess, though, and the task is a daunting one. I fear this fair city may never recover from the Tyrant's wrath, but we will do what we can, eh?

My good horse took a stone in his hoof on the road and is terribly lame. Perhaps it seems paltry, but I am rather attached to that animal. One becomes so when one's life depends on his horse. It is not like the lush pastures at home, where I can turn him out on soft ground for six months to recover. I am in hopes that he will be quite himself in time, but until then, I am on a remount that barely knows how to answer the bugle. Fortunately, I shall not have to concern myself with such a thing for the present.

I shall write something cheerful to Georgiana, but I am in earnest when I say I expect some reply from you. She is my ward as well, you know, and my mother will be asking questions of us both if she slips into a melancholy. I pray your leg is mending well and the doctors have not tortured you overmuch.

Fondly,
Richard

Miss Elizabeth Bennet to Miss Jane Bennet

28 August 1812

Jane,

Prepare yourself for a series of shocks. I shall write it quietly so our aunt's babe is not disturbed in her nursery as you read it, but you may well imagine the tone in which this piece of intelligence was conveyed to me. Ahem, let me see if I can get this right.

Netherfield is let at last!

There, did that ring authentic? Mama is in transports of ecstasy, and we hardly know the name of the person who has taken it. Supposedly, it is a family called Bingley. Well, some say it is a family, and some have it that Mr Bingley is a single gentleman of large fortune. Because every man who lets a house must be wealthy and in search of a wife, else he ought not trouble the neighbourhood with the bother of learning his name.

I think since our uncle Philips was an accessory to the transaction, we may depend at least somewhat on his intelligence, and he has quite persuaded Mama that we ought to be the first family to greet this Mr Bingley upon his arrival. She intends to be waiting on his very doorstep, but Papa maintains that he will not stir himself from his library to greet this upstart from the north. However, here comes the second shock.

Papa and I are coming to London.

The most obvious reason for this would naturally be to bring you home, since Aunt has been well delivered of her trials. Mama sniffs when doing her embroidery (she sniffs often, as you may recall) that as you have had full three months in London to catch a husband and have not yet secured one, you may as well come home and see what may be made of Mr Bingley's acquaintance. Who knows that you may not be wealthy and settled within a fortnight?

But there is another development which you may find amusing. Papa and I—well, mostly I—have still been carrying on a correspondence with our Gentleman of the Books. I have said little of him, but we delight in his letters very much. I think he must be an elderly bachelor and more infirm than not. He has written of being confined to his bed after some dreadful accident, and you know how a simple fall can lay low one of advanced years. I quite pity him.

He has been outrageously generous. It makes me wonder if he truly is on death's bed, and simply giving away his finer possessions to one who will appreciate them. I fancy some evil relations waiting to pounce on even his quills and linens upon his demise. He recently sent an entire crate of the most expensive books, and the one thing he asked in return is the loan of Papa's copy of *The History of Charles Grandison*.

Naturally we could have it sent, but Papa and I both agreed that since a journey to London is in order anyway, to spare you the discomfort of riding coach, we would deliver it in person. Due to our gentleman's indisposition, we shall probably leave the book with the footman. Although, I confess, it would be charming to have a face to put to the name. I hope our gentleman is pleasantly surprised rather than justly horrified at our audacity.

We come on Tuesday next, so shop and flirt and carry on as if your freedom were about to come to an end, because... it is.

All the love my little heart possesses,
Lizzy

Twelve

31 August 1812

B ingley,

I am afraid you will have to repair the broken dike yourself, and before winter if you are not to be troubled by flooded fields and indignant neighbours. It is unfortunate that the owner of the property refuses to make the repairs at his own expense before you take up residence, but, as you say, suitable properties are not springing up on every causeway. If this is the only fault you find in the property, it is still for the best that you took it.

I regret that I must decline your invitation once more. You know how greatly I would wish to survey your new property and congratulate you in person, but it is not possible at the moment. My physician is to come tomorrow, however, and I am confident that I shall soon be rid of these ridiculous boards strapped to my leg. With any luck, I will see you before Christmastide.

You may thank Miss Bingley on my behalf for the portrait she sent of herself to cheer Georgiana. It was very kind of her to think of sending it when she was sorting through her belongings in preparation for the move to Netherfield. I believe the portrait has been hung in the uppermost room, between those of my grandfather thrice removed and an old portrait rumoured among the servants to belong to one Mary Robinson. I expect Miss Bingley's image in that room will greatly enhance the aesthetic.

If I have not said it heartily enough before, I offer my well wishes on your new venture. I doubt not that having your own establishment will be the making of you. Do not be too hasty in trying to settle in every facet of life. What I mean by that is take care to become proficient in your role as master of the estate before you seek a mistress for it.

There is one point at which you may do me a service. You wrote that your new property is not far from the town of Meryton in Hertfordshire, I believe? I have fallen into a rather unusual correspondence with a gentleman who must be your neighbour. Perhaps when you are settled, you may tell me something of a Mr Thomas Bennet. I understand he has several daughters, but I know little more of him or his family. If you can satisfy my curiosity about what sort of man he is, I would be grateful.

Sincerely,
FD

Doctor Elton Carter to Doctor Bernard Fitzher-
bert

1 September 1812

M y esteemed Sir,

It was very kind of the prince Regent to send you to us again, with his compliments. I assure you; Mr Darcy is not ordinarily so irascible as to chase people from his bedchamber by threatening to throw vases at their heads. I am certain he meant nothing by it, for Mr Darcy has never been known to express a temper until his recent confinement. I fear my patient was in some distress over the news that his recovery is not proceeding as rapidly as he likes.

If you have not entirely washed your hands of the gentleman (and myself), I will beg you not to repeat to His Highness what Mr Darcy may have uttered about the Royal Personage under the influence of the narcotic we administered to move him. I fear Lord Matlock would have something to say to me on the matter, and it was all very innocent, as I am sure you must understand.

I am heartened by your concurrence that the flesh is, indeed, mending, and there is no longer any need to keep the limb bound. It is surely miracle enough to please anyone, even Mr Darcy, were he fully in his senses, for few are the men who do not succumb to septicaemia after such an injury. I agree that the oedema and the accompanying discomfort of injured sinews will continue to abate, and there is now no fear of blood poisoning. I have tasked the cook with keeping to bland courses, as is healthful for cooling the humours, rather than the heavily spiced beef requested by her master.

Mr Darcy's Bath chair is to be delivered today. I am in hopes that a return to mobility will do much to alleviate his low spirits. I pray you will not find it necessary to describe to strange ears the state in which you found my patient. Indeed, he does have an excellent housekeeper, but he has preferred solitude during his recovery, save for the presence of that ill-favoured dog. By the by, I do not believe he bites, but his growl is, I grant you, most intimidating. I fear even Mr Darcy's personal valet has enjoyed little admittance to his sickroom. Certainly, permitting himself to resemble his own dog is unbecoming to a man of his station.

I remain yours in humblest respect
Doctor Elton Carter

Private Diary of Miss Georgiana Darcy

1 September 1812

F itzwilliam came out of his room today for the first time since it all happened. He had ordered a Bath chair that arrived this afternoon, and so that he might move about the house, he made Carson and Giles, his valet, transfer him to his study downstairs. I do not think Doctor Carter was very pleased by that, for he said surely Fitzwilliam's leg would be injured again, but they got him carried down without mishap. Gracious, but he needs a shave! But after all the fuss of moving his bed into his study, the doctor was quite firm that Fitzwilliam ought to rest before his valet made him more presentable.

I am terribly relieved. I have been thinking of asking if I might accept Miss Bingley's invitation to Hertfordshire, though I know perfectly well that Fitzwilliam would not stand for me to go alone, and I could not abide Miss Bingley's sole attentions for more than a few days. But the house has been so very lonely. I have had no callers and no diversions—not that I could bear them, in any case, but my spirits are heavy. This has all been my fault, after all. I am so glad to have Fitzwilliam downstairs and to know that he is getting better.

However, now I fear making noise in case I should disturb him in the next room when he wishes to rest. But he has asked me to play my new piano, now that he is near enough to hear it, so I shall play this afternoon. I hope I shall be able to write that it cheered him or at least moved him out of his melancholy.

~

Fitzwilliam was, indeed, moved, but not the way I had hoped.

I was playing his favourite piece, *Robin Adair*, which he always finds bright and joyful. He was in the next room, and I knew him to be alert, so I thought it an opportune time to play. Indeed, I later learned he was trying out his new Bath chair to prepare for his shave. I had just reached the song's end and was starting over when Carson informed me that my brother had callers.

"How very strange!" I said, for not even the earl and countess are calling on him at present. He has made it very clear that none were to be admitted, save on the most urgent business. But with my brother now downstairs and feeling somewhat better, Carson asked if an exception ought to be made, for these callers had brought a gift. It was a modest-looking gentleman and a young lady, he said, and as he handles the post, their name was familiar to him as friends of my brother.

I thought perhaps I might already know them, and they must have heard me playing when they were shown in the door. Would it not be rude to turn them away, especially as they had brought a gift? I knew not what to do, so I went to greet them myself.

They were a Mr and Miss Bennet, they said. I hardly remember what the gentleman looked like, save that he seemed nearly too old to be the young lady's father, as he claimed. She, however, had quite a nice face, and I thought when she first smiled at me that I should like to have her as a friend.

But that hope was dashed, for she had hardly finished her greeting when Fitzwilliam's rotten old dog bounded out of the study to bark at her. How I despise that animal! He dashed out all frantic and slavering, with the scruff of his back standing up just so and stopped just short of snapping at Miss Bennet's hand. She dropped a book she was holding, but to her credit, she hardly screamed at all.

The worst, however, was yet to come. Fitzwilliam roared out of his study, pushed by Giles in his new wheeled contraption. He was raising his voice to that infernal beast Harold, as I have seldom heard him do in my life, and his face was still a furry nightmare, as he had not yet had his shave. I do not know what could have possessed him to order poor Giles to bring him out in such a state. As I have written, he does not seem himself. He thundered at our petrified guests most prodigiously for daring to intrude into his house uninvited.

He did not stay long in the room. I think he was terribly embarrassed when they gave him their names, for he was quite out of countenance and not fit to receive anyone. I do not like to recall the shock on his face, for it pains me even now.

I am sorry that Miss Bennet left so quickly afterward. I should have liked to know who she was and why she was giving my brother a book. I suppose now I never shall, for she took it with her when she fled the house.

Thirteen

Private Diary of Fitzwilliam Darcy

1 September 1812

I have met her at last. And, if she has any sense, I shall never see her again.
She had very fine eyes.

Mr Thomas Bennet to Mr Fitzwilliam Darcy

3 September 1812

D ear Sir,
     Please find enclosed the collection of books by Sir Walter Scott that you so kindly lent us. We do not wish to trouble you further.

    Yours & etc.
    Thomas Bennet

Miss Elizabeth Bennet to Mrs Madeline Gardiner

5 September 1812

D ear Aunt,
     Please thank my uncle for his assistance in returning the crate of books to the gentleman in Grosvenor Square. I am sure it must have cost him some trouble, and I thank you both for your consideration.
    I am still somewhat in shock that you were, in fact, familiar with the gentleman. I thought it mere jesting, but to think you grew up nearly in the shadow of his estate puts a different slant on the matter. I had not thought him so wealthy as that. His

letters were all quite unassuming. Though his house was far grander than I had expected, the man we encountered was something of an unkempt tyrant, as ill-tempered as he was ill-favoured. Are you certain he is one of the most sought-after bachelors of the *ton*? I cannot credit it.

I confess, I am terribly morose over it all. I did derive such amusement from his letters and would happily have carried on forever. If only we had not thought ourselves welcome to deliver his book in person! But it seemed just the thing, as we were to come to London. Well, I am corrected, and I feel somewhat ill over my presumption. I had come to think of Mr Darcy as a friendly, clever fellow, and even a kindred spirit who could appreciate a good book as well as a good joke.

Indeed, he did seem somewhat discomposed. It is possible that you are correct and that he would have received us as a gentleman on a better day. But even if we did arrive at an inopportune moment, there was no need to send his dog after us and declare me "not worthy of his notice." Yes, that was before he entered the room and saw us, but should that matter?

No, Aunt, I have quite done with Mr Darcy, and I shall be sorry if I ever hear his name again. I had not looked for anything beyond bookish friendship, which I value far above the poor dancing of Elliot Goulding and the ignorant chatter of John Lucas. I shall not comment on the dubious pleasure of Marcus Danforth's company at dinner. What good is such a suitor when one might have had a friend?

Please kiss baby Elinor for me and do me the good service of forgetting this humiliating episode.

E

Mr Fitzwilliam Darcy to Colonel Richard Fitzwilliam

4 September 1812

R ichard,

Indeed, I am overdue with an explanation. I shall render it on the condition that you do not charge home with pistols blazing to avenge some wrong. You are correct in deducing that it was no mere turn in Hyde Park, nor even a leap in a field that caused my current indisposition. Perhaps I shall spare you some details, as you are too distant to do much about the matter, but I lost a duel. More accurately, it was a mutual unhorsing.

I suppose it is not fair to call it a duel, for no seconds were secured, no formal challenge issued, but I was defending a lady's honour. Georgiana's, to be exact. I can almost hear your astonishment already. Yes, our innocent, child-like angel attracted the nefarious notice of none other than our old friend George Wickham. I had noticed a change of tone in her letters, and, suspecting mere low spirits, I determined to pay her a visit in Ramsgate. Fortunately for us all, I arrived at the same moment as the carriage that was to carry them away to heaven-knows-where.

It is bad enough that she, who has been raised to know better, was persuaded to an elopement, but Wickham's betrayal inspired a rage in me I had never known I could possess. When he leapt to the back of the nearest saddle horse, I mounted mine and gave chase. You recall how he used to ruin maidens and then flee the very grasps of their indignant fathers? I did not mean to let him escape this time, so I caught him up as he was running across the lowlands, and we had a fearful scuffle on the backs of two racing horses. I had the upper hand until we came round a blind corner and passed almost instantly under an oak tree. He was struck down by the head, and I was swept off in such a way that my boot caught in the iron, and I was dragged for about ten yards.

I was told later that he probably suffered a concussion but was able to escape. I do not know where he is now, nor have I the means to search him out. My helplessness in that regard has done little for my present peace of mind.

Poor Georgiana bore the trouble of finding a surgeon and bringing me to London, and it was no easy feat. In fact, if it were not for the fact that Giles had attended me to Ramsgate, I am certain I could not have made the journey. I was considerably more damaged than a simple broken bone. It was an open break, and you know well the complications that arise from such an injury.

I also suffered two fractured ribs and several sprains and abrasions. My right cheek was so swollen I could not see out of that eye for several days (though that mattered little, for I was senseless most of the time), and I shudder to recall the horror of my right leg when I regained consciousness. Carter was ready to remove it below the knee at once. It was only by making a brute and a monster of myself, feared by everyone I encountered, that I kept it. I regret to say I succeeded a little too well in that last endeavour, but I shall not write more of that here.

Georgiana blames herself, and I am hardly in a position to reassure her. How can I, when every moment she spends in my company she is reminded of that terrible day? I am at a loss about how to help her, for naturally I cannot reveal these events to Lady Matlock or any of her friends. I must find a new companion for her, but I do not think it proper to interview such a woman in my present state.

There, now you have the full account. I trust you will now send a dozen outraged letters trying to find Wickham and bring him to justice, but I would advise you to spare yourself the trouble. The last thing we need atop everything else is a scandal. I will find George Wickham soon enough. His debts always catch up with him.

Do keep yourself safe. Though the worst may be behind me, I am still far from recovered. In my more sombre moments, I confess to myself that it shall be a long time, if ever, before I am on two feet again. One of us, at least, must walk our girl down the aisle to the right sort of husband someday.

FD

Fourteen

5 September 1812

D arcy,

Her Ladyship has requested the honour of Georgiana's company as she waits on callers next week. I think it will do my niece much good, and I urge you to accept on Georgiana's behalf. You cannot keep her sitting outside your sick room, either for your well-being or for hers.

I am greatly heartened by the news from Carter that your leg is improving. I hope you will forgive me for interfering with your steward, but matters did look rather dire. I was trying to protect your interests, as well as those of Georgiana—a thing you had not properly done.

Pray consider this a warning to secure the future of the estate by marrying as soon as may be. Lady Matlock has arranged a list of suitable candidates, some of whom will doubtless meet Georgiana when she comes to us.

I look forward to your reply.
Ralph Fitzhugh, Lord Matlock

Miss Elizabeth Bennet to Miss Charlotte Lucas

7 September 1812

C harlotte,

No, we have not yet been introduced to our new neighbours at Netherfield, though Mama has been lamenting night and day that Papa will not stir from his library to present himself. For my part, I can bear the distress of not encountering another full-of-himself gentleman from the north. No, I do not intend to explain that remark.

Did your brother truly task you with asking me to dance at the next Assembly for him? You may tell John that I anticipate being otherwise engaged for every set, even if that means you and I are sitting in the corner together and whispering over the gowns worn by our new neighbours. How many sisters did you say this Bingley character had? Far too many, I say, for we have not enough gentlemen of our own in Meryton. How dare they come to poach more of them!

Marcus Danforth called this morning to advise us that he was summoned by his wealthy aunt to return to Featherington or some-such place. I only fancied the name of her estate because he seems so very feathery in the head, but Mary is quite broken up about his departure. She has been playing dirges for the past hour. Her grief, however, pales to Mama's, who nearly sent Hill out to sabotage his carriage. Had she done so, Prince George would no doubt have had some sport.

Ah, and to answer your last question, no, I am not put out by anything in particular. I am sorry you noted something in my countenance when we came to tea yesterday. I shall take care only to smile and laugh from now on. I shall see you tomorrow.

E

Mr Fitzwilliam Darcy to Miss Elizabeth Bennet and Mr Thomas Bennet

8 September 1812

B e not alarmed, madam, that I shall come at you again with a barking dog and the manners of a cave dweller. My humblest apologies are insufficient to the shame I feel at the way I presented myself.

Miss Bennet, I hope you and your father will forgive my presumption in writing to you again. For a week, my conscience has smitten me until I at last took up my pen to seek forgiveness. My honour demands that an apology be made, thus the letter shall be written. Whether you choose to read it shall be your affair.

I had not long been in correspondence with you before I noted a peculiar affinity of mind. Your sense of humour I found engaging, your wit worthy of respect. I fear I might have carried on thus indefinitely, though I know full well the impracticality of it. Perhaps it is for the better that we cease writing altogether, but I would not sever ties with you while you had just cause to think so ill of me.

Perhaps I will first apologize for Harold. He is a Scottish sheep herding dog who was gifted to my father ten years ago by one of his tenants. Upon my father's death, Harold switched his allegiance to me. He is old and stubborn now and was never possessed of fashionable breeding or outstanding beauty. In fact, there are many in my circle who have urged me to get rid of him, or at least keep him secreted away in the country, for he is not a fine hunter or a pointer, but a farmer's working dog. But that is the crux of it—I care little for appearances. I value creatures of substance and honesty, be they man or beast, and a more loyal companion than Harold, a man could never wish for.

I am afraid his protective instincts have been on full display since my accident. He scarcely permits even my own sister to visit me, and he has a special distaste for the surgeon and doctor whose attentions have so often elicited responses of pain on my part. The day you called, I had only just removed downstairs to enjoy the freedoms of a Bath chair during the rest of my recuperation, and his poor nerves were suffering greatly. I hope he did not frighten you too badly.

And now I come to myself. How shall I make amends for my behaviour? If I claim I asked my valet to push me out in the hall merely to recall my inhospitable dog, it reflects poorly on my temper, but the truth, I confess, looks even worse than that. The truth was that I believed your father's voice in the drawing room was my doctor, come to torment me again, and I had enough of his ministrations for the day. I fear I have made a menace of myself to that poor man, and I wonder that he will still have aught to do with me. When I spoke those unprepossessing things as I was being wheeled through the hall, I'd never any notion my words would fall on a lady's ears.

No, not just a lady. I had counted you a friend, Miss Bennet. That is of far greater worth to me than the title of "lady," and I hope your father will forgive my familiarity in calling you such. I have valued his letters as well, but yours were the ones that brought pleasure when all else was pain. It has been a season of various trials, but the pair of you gave me cheer when little else could.

I am sorry that you felt it necessary to return the books. I hope you will accept this second offering of them, this time with no requests or strings attached. Merely receive them with my appreciation. And now, so that I may cause no more distress to your spirits or harm to Miss Bennet's reputation, I shall call an end to my correspondence.

May God bless you both,
Fitzwilliam Darcy

.

Fifteen

10 September 1812

M r Darcy,
    I wished to apprise you of matters at Pemberley. I have attached the final yield totals for the wheat and potatoes, and this season's beef shall be in next week. Mrs Reynolds reports that the stores of herbs and preserves are put up and the apples this year were especially sweet. I am pleased to report that the well water has remained high all season, and your design for a rain runoff on the livestock barns has been implemented.

This year's foals are weaned and pastured on the South slope. Jeffers has begun stabling them by night, and he says all are growing well. You asked him to pay special attention to the bay colt, and he agrees that the bay is the fleetest of them all. He might do well if you were to send him to Newmarket when he is older.

All is proceeding apace for the season. We are in hopes that you will soon be well enough to make the journey back to us. Mrs Reynolds has fitted a room on the first level of the house for your comfort, and I have taken the liberty of securing a low cart that might be used to travel about the estate. I thought Miss Georgiana's former riding pony might serve well in this capacity, but of course, I leave that to you.

There is one more peculiar matter, which I am sure is of little import, but I shall mention it in case I am wrong. A letter arrived addressed to you from an offended innkeeper in Canterbury, who claims you owe him a deal of money and that you had pledged yourself to the debt. It cannot be possible, of course, for he avows you stayed at his inn for a fortnight this summer and drank a prodigious amount of his ale. I knew the dates to be just after your accident, and you were, therefore, in London all that time.

I would have merely discarded it, but a week after the first letter arrived, a second came like it. This was from Rochester. I know you are not a man to leave debts behind, so I know not what to conclude. I enclosed both letters for you to examine and dispatch as you see fitting.

Respectfully,
John Talbot

Colonel Richard Fitzwilliam to Fitzwilliam Darcy

30 September 1812

D arcy,

I am coming home. Look for me on the next tide.

R

Charles Bingley to Fitzwilliam Darcy

2 October 1812

D arcy,

I cannot tell you what a delight Hertfordshire is! I have scarcely settled, and already I have attended a local Assembly and been introduced to three and twenty neighbours and their families. I suppose one might say four and twenty, save that I have not yet met this Mr Bennet you tasked me to tell you of. I have met his daughters, though. More on that in a moment.

As you always ask after business, I shall first take care to inform you that I have ordered repairs to all the little matters about the house and property that wanted attention. The barns are now snug for winter, the ditches all in order, a few little bits of plaster on the house mended, and I have even had the honour of aiding a tenant in need when his wife took to her sickbed after a difficult confinement. I quite think I have outdone myself, and I am certain I have left nothing amiss.

There, are you not pleased to hear it? I was more apprehensive than I wished to confess, taking this venture on without your direct guidance, but perhaps I was not so ill-equipped as I feared. I still desire for you to come to Netherfield when you may, but of course, your recuperation and your own estate's affairs must come before mine.

The one troubling aspect of my present circumstances is Caroline. She has been impossible to please, and I have nearly given up trying. I think she would have managed tolerably well had we guests for her to fawn over, but as we do not, she has proved nearly intolerable. I thought she would refuse to attend the Assembly last evening, for she had such a fearful row with Louisa and sent her poor lady's maid out to the hothouse for at least four sets of roses for her shoes. But she did attend after all that, though what amusement she found there, I cannot say. I was far more agreeably engaged.

Darcy, I have met an angel. I am quite pleased you said something about your friend Mr Bennet, for I was looking for an introduction to the gentleman. He was not in attendance last evening, but his wife and daughters were. I can say little of Mrs Bennet, for I was instantly swept away by the clearest, sky-blue eyes I have ever seen, accompanied by the smile of... well, an angel. Miss Jane Bennet is like the sweet waters of the Italian sea—cool and fresh and soothing to the senses. She was my anchor all evening, the quiet centre of the room no matter where I turned. Aye, I danced with her twice, though gentlemen were scarce, and we drew more than a few whispers.

I danced with each of her sisters as well, though only one of them provided stimulating conversation. Miss Elizabeth was second in both age and beauty to her sister. She is sharp whereas Miss Bennet is soft, and clever where her sister is mild, but I enjoyed my dance with her very much. I mean to present myself to Mr Bennet soon so that I may see more of his family.

I do hope your leg is healing well. Caroline says Miss Georgiana has been brief in her letters, but she informs us you have acquired a Bath chair. That is excellent news! Should you find it preferable to leave London for a time, but Pemberley proves too far to journey, you may consider yourself most welcome at Netherfield. We will do what we can to make you comfortable.

Fondly,
CB

Lady Catherine to Mr Fitzwilliam Darcy

5 October 1812

Nephew,

I have a letter from Colonel Fitzwilliam that he has been granted leave for the winter. I told you, did I not, that my influence carries far? I have written to the general that my nephew must be released from his obligations for a time to satisfy the needs of his family. The army must and shall yield on this point, for what is England and why is she worth defending if matters at home are not attended to?

I understand you have availed yourself of a Bath chair and are mobile once again. Very well. I still do not know why a cane would not suffice, but if you insist on making an unseemly fuss, then so it shall be. I shall expect you to Rosings at Christmastide, for you know how difficult it is for Anne to travel any distance at this time of year. There are matters we must settle, and I am quite in agreement with the earl on this point.

(Hereon affixed the great seal of)
Lady Catherine de Bourgh

Sixteen

7 October 1812

My lord,

Please convey my appreciation to Lady Walton and Miss Emmaline for their kindness to Miss Darcy. The Countess of Matlock has been exceedingly gracious, and I am gratified to know that my sister has delighted in receiving callers with her.

At this time, I must ask that such friendly encounters take place only under the guidance of Lady Matlock. Miss Darcy is not prepared to receive callers at home, nor am I presently equipped to welcome guests. I thank you for your generous offer of interviewing a lady's companion so that visits between Miss Emmaline and Miss Darcy may resume here, but I believe it is better if Miss Darcy relies on Lady Matlock for such assistance.

I regret that Lady Walton and Miss Emmaline were startled by my dog. I am sorry to say the ladies are not the first unexpected callers to be treated to his winsome ways, nor are they likely to be the last. I do not intend to "deal with him" as you suggested, but I shall consider other means of ascertaining that he will not strike fear into the hearts of any more ladies. For the present, I shall keep him close to my chair.

Yours most respectfully,
Fitzwilliam Darcy

Mr John Talbot to Mr Fitzwilliam Darcy

12 October 1812

D ear Sir,
    I am sorry to trouble you, but you said in your last reply that I ought to forward any more strange correspondence at once. I have received a third letter requesting payment for an extended stay at the Lion's Gate Inn in the town of Hertford. Once again, the innkeeper swears you told him to forward the amount due to the steward at Pemberley—that person being myself—and that the bill would be paid forthwith.

I can only conclude someone is masquerading as you and running up impressive tabs as he does so. Sir, I hesitate to suggest it, but perhaps you have already reached the same conclusion as I. If our suspicions be accurate, Mr George Wickham is somewhere in Hertfordshire.

I have written a draft to cover the expenses, as you directed in your last letter. Unless advised to do otherwise, I shall handle subsequent requests in the same manner, but please indicate to me your wishes. I should like to hire an investigator to search out the gentleman using your name, but of course, that is yours to decide.

Respectfully,
John Talbot

Miss Elizabeth Bennet to Mr Fitzwilliam Darcy

13 October 1812

D ear sir,
    My father has reluctantly agreed to send you a letter on my behalf one last time. He is of the opinion that we should not write, as you stated a preference to let our acquaintance drop. I am of the opinion that some of his favourite books will disappear if he refuses to let me have my share in the conversation.

I cannot read the remorse in your letter without doing something to assuage it. I bear the responsibility for setting upon you uninvited. My sister Jane had been in Town and was ready to come home, and it was I who had the notion to use the opportunity to call on you in person. I know that is not the way "things are done." Perhaps I shall blame my fascination with the man behind the letters for thinking we might be welcome, for I derived full as much enjoyment from yours as you claim to have done from mine.

That aside, I do not think your dog is homely or vicious. In fact, there was an instant there when he seemed most becoming. It was just after he terrorized me and just before you rolled into the room behind him, when he ceased his barking to sniff the book I had dropped and to wag his tail. I do not think a dog who happily sniffs books can be bad. And any creature who will comfort and guard his master when indisposed is one worthy of a soft pillow and many affectionate pats on the head. So, pray, do not feel badly on account of Harold.

I do hope you are recovering. I know not what manner of accident you met with, but after all you had written, I am pleased that you now have some measure of mobility again. I hope it cheers you and your prospects are now not so gloomy as they had been. Perhaps you were a *bit* of a brute as you exploded into the drawing room that day, but the Black Dwarf, you were not. I should say you were hardly even on the scale of Bois-Guilbert, for you never even issued orders to have us thrown into your dungeon. You see, I can laugh about the matter now. I am only sorry for the disturbance we caused you.

Pray, give my regards to Miss Darcy. You never mentioned a sister, but I was pleased to meet her, however briefly. I hope you will tell her I am dreadfully sorry for the fright we gave her. And do the same for Harold.

My very best wishes for your health and happiness,

EB

Mr Fitzwilliam Darcy to Mr Charles Bingley

14 October 1812

B ingley,
I find myself entirely restless and dull in London. For reasons I shall not detail here, I believe it would do me much good if I were to accept your invitation to stay a month in Hertfordshire.

It is no small thing I ask of you, for I am hardly a proper guest. I shudder to think of the trouble involved in moving from place to place, and the four-hour carriage ride will be little short of Dante's Seventh Circle. But should I survive, I have no doubt of being far more comfortable than if I remain here.

My surgeon, Elton Carter, has insisted upon accompanying me in the carriage, but he will return to London at once. As I have been far from the ideal patient, I am attempting to make amends and become somewhat more docile for the good doctor. That docility does not, I fear, extend so far as to exclude Harold from the journey. If it is not too much trouble, I shall bring him, for he is old and does not suffer himself to be parted from me easily.

Lastly, I have acceded to Georgiana's entreaties. She is begging to come, particularly as her best alternative is to remain with Lady Matlock. I am not so heartless as to leave my sister to the tender mercies of all the ladies of the *ton* who call incessantly on the countess. I trust Miss Bingley will also be cheered to have another guest.

I hope I have not abused your hospitality with the many demands my presence must and shall surely impose upon you. I blame it on my eagerness to see all you have accomplished, and to meet some of your neighbours. You may look for me on Friday.

Yours,
FD

Seventeen

Miss Elizabeth Bennet to Mrs Madeline Gardiner

16 October 1812

Aunt,

Mr Darcy has come here! My fingers are still shaking from the shock of it, so I shall measure my breaths until I can command myself. It is difficult to concentrate with so much caterwauling as is carrying on downstairs, for Lydia claims to have made her own conquest in Meryton. But let me tell you about Mr Darcy. First, I must tell you about Jane.

I told you, did I not, that Jane was quite five times prettier than the rest of us? It seems Mr Bingley agreed, and well he might, for he is not a stupid man, and he has both eyes fixed in their proper places. We met him at the Assembly a fortnight ago, and he caused a stir by dancing twice with Jane. I believe I may have written that much to you last week.

For her part, Jane goes utterly silent and can only smile when Mr Bingley's name is mentioned, by which I know beyond doubt she has tumbled bonnet over petticoats for him. I heartily approve, for he can put together more than two sentences and he does not pick his teeth. On the whole, he is a perfectly acceptable specimen of his sex.

There, that is ungenerous, for Mr Bingley is quite an affable man, and gentlemanly in every way. And that brings me to the sort of associations he forms. Aunt, he has been close friends with our Mr Darcy for many years! Such a friend is he that Mr Darcy has come to stay at Netherfield, though his leg is not fully mended, and he is confined to a Bath chair for some while longer. I ask you; how many friends do you have upon whom you could feel comfortable imposing so?

But I am getting ahead of myself again. Mr Bingley's sisters are not the kind and generous souls he is, but they had taken some interest in Jane. I believe Miss Bingley was bored, but she invited Jane to dine with her last Wednesday, and then this morning, Jane and I were both invited to tea. Just as we were about to take our leave, a large carriage pulled up in the drive.

I think Miss Bingley was as shocked by Mr Darcy's arrival as I was, for she upset her cup and was forced to retire upstairs to change quickly. That left Jane and me, with Mrs Hurst, standing beside Mr Bingley to greet the newcomers.

Aunt, he is quite fetching. Handsome, even. Nay... he is a sculptor's masterpiece.

I had not noted this when I met him before, but I believe you now when you say he has to lock his doors at night. You know very well I am not the girl to swoon for a strong jaw or a brooding brow or an enigmatic gaze, but the gentleman has all three. Is that not monstrous unfair? To add to it, he has all his teeth (I saw them when he smiled at me) and the poor man is temporarily in such a physical condition to make the heart of any feeling person pity him. It was a fall from his horse, he said, and his boot caught in the iron. It was a terrible break, of the sort that kills or cripples most men.

Oh, but Mr Darcy is not most men. Miss Bingley swears he has a fortune to rival Midas, and she has declared him to be nearly her own property. The poor fellow! It made me want to shield him like a lost waif. But apparently, he does not need a woman's protection, despite his present affliction, and I daresay he has a strong grip. He had to, for he was holding back his dog from barking at Miss Bingley when she rushed back downstairs in a fresh gown and tried to fawn over him. I think Harold and I could be friends. I ought to introduce him to Prince George.

So, there you have it. I am in a woeful fix, for I had sworn off corresponding with Mr Darcy because I had such a tendency to let my pen run ahead of propriety. Papa would laugh over my letters in one moment, then swear I was bound for ruin the next, but he always posted them. I did promise him after the last that I would have nothing more to do with Mr Darcy, and now, here the gentleman is.

Do you think I shall be able to meet with him as common and indifferent acquaintances? Or shall I blurt out something unsuitable about Sir Walter Scott and reveal all my scandalous history with an unmarried gentleman?

You do not need to answer that.

Your most prodigiously flustered
E

*Mr Fitzwilliam Darcy to Colonel Richard
Fitzwilliam*

19 October 1812

R ichard,

I know not when you will arrive, for I assume "the next tide" was merely a euphemism for "when I can get leave." It was not necessary for you to race back to England, but as there seemed to be nothing I could do to prevent you coming, I will simply thank you. I am sending this to Matlock House, for I assume you will go first to pay your respects to Her Ladyship, your mother. There is no purpose in you coming to Darcy House, for I am no longer in London.

Bingley has let a property in Hertfordshire, and he has been pressing me to accept his invitation to stay whenever I felt I could travel. I ought not to have attempted the journey yet, for the discomfort of the carriage ride was beyond even what I had feared. My surgeon swears I have set back my recovery by at least a month. Suffice to say, I shall not be attempting a removal in the near future. Little matter, for I have reasons enough to be content here.

Georgiana has come with me, as I am certain by now Her Ladyship will have told you. These last two days, the demands of being in company have meant that I have also seen more of her than I had almost the entire three months previous. I am ashamed that I left her so long to herself while I cursed my loneliness in my own chambers. Naturally, it could not have been helped at first, but I was not at death's door all that while. I could have done more for her just by welcoming her presence, even as I wracked my brain for ways to help her.

But that is in the past. I have other matters to discuss with you when you arrive. Firstly, I have cause to believe George Wickham is somewhere near at hand. At the suggestion of my steward, who has been the unhappy manager of some of Wickham's debts, I have hired an investigator to search him out. I expect news at almost any moment.

There is more I would tell you about why I am so suddenly come to Hertfordshire, knowing all the trouble and pain such a removal must cost, but I will save that for a private conversation. I shall simply ask you to ponder the very great pleasure bestowed by a pair of fine eyes in the face of a pretty woman.

Properly humbled,
FD

Private Diary of Mr Fitzwilliam Darcy

19 October 1812

I have met her again. Twice, now, for she happened to be calling at Netherfield the day I arrived, and she came again today with her elder sister and her father. At last, we have had a proper introduction. I had formerly called her Miss Bennet, but now that I know her place in her family, I call her Miss Elizabeth.

Elizabeth. It suits her—a name of strength and dignity and honour, yet it floats on a man's sigh like the dreamy first breath of spring drifts over the Peaks. I am afraid I have sighed her name often.

I startled her by my arrival last Friday. Bingley was thoughtful, more so than I had given him credit for, to make the arrangements for our stay without alerting Miss Bingley. Perhaps it was inconsiderate to *her*, but my relief at not being set upon the moment we exited the carriage could not be measured. And by an odd twist of fate, it was not Miss Bingley standing in the hall to greet us, but Elizabeth. Elizabeth Bennet, she of the saucy tongue and the sparkling eyes. And a smile that speaks of some secret amusement that I long to share.

Is it possible that she is everything she seems? I admired her mind long ago, but now I admire all the rest of her, and I cannot look away. I believe my favourite vantage was when Miss Bingley persuaded her to "take a turn about the room." She has a light and intoxicating way of walking.

Perhaps one day, I shall walk beside her.

Eighteen

Miss Charlotte Lucas to Elizabeth Bennet

21 October 1812

Y ou have been very sly with me, my friend.

Papa called on Mr Bingley yesterday to welcome his guest, Mr Darcy, to the neighbourhood. While there, Papa learned that Mr Darcy had brought a sister with him, so Mama and I thought it fitting that we should call on her and Miss Bingley and Mrs Hurst today. For, naturally, if one wants to learn about a gentleman, there is no more fitting place to start than with his sister.

I had meant to be the one to give you all the intelligence of him, but I find you have the advantage of me! By the by, Miss Darcy is quiet, much like Jane, I fancy. She seemed pleased to meet us, but a little uncertain of herself. That all changed the moment your name crossed my lips. She brightened at once and began asking more of you.

And so did Mr Darcy, who was on the other side of the room playing chess with Mr Bingley. He went so far as to have his chair wheeled closer so he could ask me whether I liked to read and to encourage me to come again—with you, of course—to call on Miss Darcy. I think Miss Bingley was very put out when he said that, but there was nothing she could do about it but smile and second the invitation.

I daresay, Lizzy, you seem to have made an impression on the gentleman. I hope you did not tease him too much. You ought to take my advice and be nice to this one. So, are you free for tea the day after tomorrow?

On another note, surely you have heard our younger sisters going on and on about certain officers of the militia? Mama said we should have a few of them to dinner next week, particularly this Mr Wickham they are all so charmed by. And what is this Maria tells me about a cousin come to stay with you? Mr Collins, is it? I shall demand a full accounting when I see you next.

Charlotte

Mr Thomas Bennet to Mr Edward Gardiner

23 October 1812

E dward,

Mrs Bennet is most eager for another trip to Town to examine all manner of feminine finery. You may well imagine the cause, as I am certain you have heard by now of the two young stags in residence at Netherfield. I daresay Mrs Bennet is a keener huntress with her wiles and machinations than any noble ever was with his dogs and flintlock. I ought to pity the gentlemen, but unless I miss my guess, they do not desire my pity.

I beg you to spare me the trouble of another trip to London by promising to come at Christmas. I believe I could coax Mrs Bennet into delaying her shopping if you were to come to us, hopefully with a few selections of lace and ribbon to appease her. 'Twill also incentivize my present house guest to take his leave before next spring.

Perhaps I have said little of William Collins. He is the son of my estranged uncle, and due to the odd fortunes of life, it is he who shall inherit Longbourn one day. He has come, he says, to "extend an olive branch," but also to look over my daughters for a future wife. I might let him have Mary, if she liked him, but Jane and Lizzy are far too good for him and Kitty and Lydia far too silly. I have had much sport in watching him try to charm Lizzy, though. That mongrel pup of hers has redeemed himself somewhat in my eyes, for he growls at Collins whenever he comes near her.

You are missing out on the most diverting courtship dances I have ever witnessed. Collins is merely the appetizer (and I've no doubt he shall return to Kent disappointed in his quest). The main course is taking place over at Netherfield. Bingley is a fine enough chap, and Jane seems to be pleased with him, though I think I shall faint if either of them works up the nerve to declare their feelings. But Darcy, now there is a man worth observing.

Today, I called on the gentlemen at Netherfield, and enjoyed a pleasant hour of chess with Darcy. He is clever, well-spoken, and he bested me with little effort, for it was obvious that his mind was not on the game. He thinks himself sly, no doubt, but he cannot tear his eyes from my Lizzy, who was across the room with the ladies. She and Mr Darcy have been in company four or five times now, I believe, and his interest is becoming clear to everyone.

For her part, she laughs with unusual spirit and takes inordinate pains with the styling of her hair. I cannot say what will come of it, for gentlemen of Mr Darcy's station are rarely known to trouble themselves with girls of small dowries, but I shall say this much. They can argue for hours together about the same books, and they both have an affinity for homely canines. Which, do you think, shall cross the other in love? Or shall I be welcoming him as a son before year's end? I have a smuggled bottle of Scotch to place on the wager if you will take me up on it.

In good cheer,
Thomas

Private Diary of Mr Fitzwilliam Darcy

2 November 1812

I am a fool. I know it very well.

I have never done a foolish thing in my life, but now all I can think is how to lure Elizabeth to Netherfield more often. A woman I have seen but a handful of times! Father, if I should ever have to give an accounting to you of my actions, know that good sense and decorum only carry a man so far. A woman who can make him laugh, who can challenge his mind, and who will freely forgive when offended is a treasure worth moving mountains to gain.

To all these virtues, I shall add that Harold approves of her. He let her stroke his head and even presented his belly for a rub, which she merrily rendered. Georgiana likes her as well, but with no disrespect to my dear sister, I trust Harold's appraisal of characters more than hers. Perhaps one day, Elizabeth's influence may contribute to Georgiana's wisdom.

Am I presumptuous? Indeed, I am, but my thoughts have strayed far beyond the quaint friendship I shared with a faceless maid until now, I picture her plundering my library at Pemberley as freely as she would wish. I would hear her laugh—the one I could only imagine when she was merely a pen on the page—and I would gather her into my arms each night if she permitted me that liberty. She is as warm and lively and tart as I ever hoped.

And she holds me in no awe, which fascinates me all the more. Today she set me down righteously over a most entertaining debate, and I believe I will seek a way to provoke her "courage to rise" again the next time we meet. How should I, who always prided myself on reason and purpose, lose my head and heart to such a woman?

My understanding has altered fundamentally, and, I say, for the better. No longer do I desire a wife of fashion and breeding, whose name would look handsome beside mine in the registry. I want a woman whose hand fits into mine through life's troubles, and now I know something of them. I can thank heaven now for sitting me down for a time, because I have learnt to cling to only that which will remain steadfast.

But I do long to walk again, and beside *her* if I may. I doubt my surgeon would give his leave, but I mean to test my leg to see if it can bear my weight. If matters progress as I hope, I should like to propose to Elizabeth one day, standing beside her like a man.

Ah, yes, I am in the middle of it already, and I scarcely know how I began! But I believe it was when she first made me smile.

Nineteen

Miss Elizabeth Bennet to Mrs Madeline Gardiner

10 November 1812

A unt,

I shall despise Mr Darcy forever.

Can you believe that fiend had the audacity to say he did not like *Evelina*? And then he dared risk my ire by comparing the *Romance of the Forest* to moralistic nursery rhymes! I cannot decide if he is in earnest or if he is only teasing me. Charlotte said he was smiling most indecently when I defended my favourite books.

But I do not think I can trust Charlotte's opinion of men at all, for she has set her cap for my odious cousin. A house of one's own is all fine and well, but I could not suffer a lifetime bound to a boot-licking simpleton like Mr Collins. Nothing but the deepest love shall persuade me to matrimony. And so, I shall forever live with only Prince George for company.

Lydia fancies herself nearly betrothed to an officer of the militia. He had the poor judgment to cross her path in town and to pick up the handkerchief she had dropped, and now she has fairly claimed him for her own. He is a Mr Wickham, and no one seems to know much about him but that he appears very well off among his peers and he can smile the stockings off any girl within five miles. Save for me, of course. Prince George does not care for him. But let him keep paying his compliments so prettily as he has done, and I might just forget about opinionated mutts and cryptic Mr Darcys and permit Mr Wickham to lead me in the *Allemande* at the next Assembly.

It is a pity Mr Darcy will not be able to dance soon. Perhaps never again. I would sigh about that, but I cannot altogether decide if I would accept a dance with him. No doubt he would contrive to irritate me to puckishness, and I would rise to the occasion because I always do, and then we would not be dancing at all but bickering about something silly and having an outrageously splendid time all the while others tried to dance around us. So, I probably should never try to dance with Mr Darcy.

He did something peculiar the other day, and it concerned that Mr Wickham that Lydia is so fond of. All my family were calling at Netherfield and Lydia (who has no grace whatsoever) began to pester Mr Bingley to host a ball. Everyone else was tactful enough to know why Mr Bingley will not do so (in deference to Mr Darcy) but she complained she wanted to dance with Mr Wickham and make every other girl jealous of her. I was mortified!

But Mr Darcy went sheet white. He and I had been quarrelling most pleasantly about a particular poem (I cannot recall which) when he suddenly looked like a man who is dyspeptic. Terribly odd! He ceased talking altogether, and his jaw was clenched as if in anger. I was the only one stupid enough or bold enough to ask him what the matter was, and he made some curt response—not impolite, but scarcely escaping it—and asked to be wheeled out of the room.

He came back just before we were all to leave and was quite himself again. He even asked if I might consider escorting his sister in the garden on the morrow, as he has been unable to do so. I agreed, and we parted as we always do.

If you wish to know what I mean by "as we always do," I am afraid I cannot describe it without sounding ridiculous. He is a proud man, and one can tell how greatly it vexes him that he cannot stand to his feet and bow over a lady's hand. But he does what is better if you ask me. He smiles.

Oh, yes, gentlemen do smile. But not this one. His resting countenance is the most severe expression you would ever imagine, but when engaged in a conversation that pleases him, his face is radiant, like a babe having its first taste of sugar. By the by, I have been remiss in asking about Elinor and the children. I do hope they will all come at Christmas! Tell them Cousin Elizabeth will have a sugar mouse for each of them.

I will seal this now and blow out my candle because Jane is trying to sleep. Tomorrow morning, my sisters and I will walk to Meryton with Mr Collins (and Charlotte, no doubt), and then Jane and I will call on Miss Darcy in the afternoon.

Your
Occasionally exasperated, frequently embarrassed, and entirely fascinated with a man in a Bath chair
Lizzy

PS Mr Darcy does have a very nice smile when he employs it.
E

PPS, I did not mean that bit about never dancing with him.
If he should ask, that is. But I doubt he ever shall.

Probably not, anyway.

No, I am quite decided. It would be a dreadful idea. And
anyway, Miss Bingley would be very put out that he did not
ask her first.

Lizzy

Mr Fitzwilliam Darcy to Colonel Fitzwilliam

6 November 1812

R ichard,

I expect you almost any day—in fact, I am surprised
you have not already landed, breathless and dripping at
Netherfield's doorstep. But I shall send this off in case you are
not already en route from London. I have definitive news of
George Wickham.

He has enlisted in the militia, which is stationed in Hertfordshire for the winter. My investigator has followed the path
left by Wickham since that fateful day in Ramsgate, and he
has added two more inns which claim a balance owed for
Wickham's stay and the ale he drank. Again, he gave my name.
I cannot fathom why, for surely, he would know I would find
him out, unless he believed I was too indisposed to investigate

the matter and my steward so incompetent that he would simply pay the bill without looking into it. Or perhaps Wickham wanted me to find him, as if he was taunting me? I choose to think he merely enjoyed the finer rooms and spirits he could command with my name than with his own.

It appears he decided his luck in that way was about to run out. For once he came to Hertfordshire, he abruptly changed tactics. It is unclear whether he sought out the militia as a means to survive, or if he was merely persuaded to it by another of the officers. He seems to be very popular among the ranks, and I do not wonder why. It is reported that he often lost at cards and flashed a good deal of coin when he first enlisted. No doubt it was the last of the money from Georgiana's reticule that disappeared with him.

I have also learned that he is worming his way into the affections of the neighbourhood. Many are the daughters of the local gentry who would swoon at his feet, and you know as well as I that he cannot be trusted with a swooning young gentlewoman. I could not forgive myself if any of them were ruined, and I did nothing to prevent it. There is one family in particular that might be vulnerable, but I shall say no more of that in a letter.

Wickham must be stopped. I mean to call for the local magistrate on Monday and have him thrown into debtor's prison, unless by some miracle you should happen to arrive before then with a better plan.

FD

PS
Today I walked across my chambers without Giles's help. I had forgotten how tall I was.
FD

*Miss Georgiana Darcy to Misses Jane and Eliz-
abeth Bennet*

7 November 1812

M y dear friends,

The most wonderful thing has happened! My cousin Richard, the one I told you about who was serving His Majesty in Portugal, has come to Netherfield!

I did not know to expect him, but Fitzwilliam seems very pleased to see him. He arrived almost as we were retiring last evening, and his horse looked as if he had galloped all the way from London. (I say that as a jest, for he told me himself he changed horses three times.)

I am sure Richard will vastly cheer my brother, though he has already been so much pleasanter here at Netherfield than he was in London. All is finally coming right! I am most eager to introduce you to my cousin. It is a pity you were here only this afternoon and missed seeing him by mere hours. I am sure you would like him, for everyone does.

I wish we could all come to services in Meryton this morning and sit in the pew just behind yours. Fitzwilliam believes that very soon, perhaps even by next week, he may be able to manage it. I caught him leaning on Richard's shoulder last evening and testing the strength of his leg, and I overheard him telling my cousin that he had been walking a few steps here and there for a couple of weeks. I do not think Doctor Carter would approve, but I do.

But do not tell Miss Bingley, please.

Until I see you next,
Georgiana Darcy

Colonel Richard Fitzwilliam to Colonel Andrew Forster

9 November 1812

D ear sir,
   I believe we have been introduced before; five years ago, when I was serving under Captain Lowrey in the Regulars. You were most helpful in the matter of that troublesome lieutenant.

I have another lieutenant to call to your attention, only this one is serving under your command. I have just returned from the Continent on a special leave, and I came to stay at Netherfield Park only yesterday. My cousin, Fitzwilliam Darcy of Pemberley in Derbyshire, is presently a guest here as well, and due to some issues of form, he has been paying the debts of an old acquaintance, George Wickham.

This Wickham is well known to our family and has a long history of leaving debts, both in trade and debts of honour. Darcy has been seeking him to settle accounts, and upon my arrival last evening, he informed me that Mr Wickham has enlisted in your regiment.

Darcy has a careful record of all Wickham's unpaid bills, some of which were incurred under Darcy's own name. He is prepared to have the lieutenant thrown into a debtor's prison until his ways be mended and his debts paid. However, I suggested an alternative action that he has agreed to, should it prove palatable to yourself. I would not short the Crown of able-bodied fighters when we need every man to defend England. But nor does it seem prudent to leave such a rascal at large to burden shopkeepers and his fellow officers with promises of repayment that will never come.

There is evidence at hand that this Mr Wickham once stole nearly a dozen books belonging to his patron George Darcy—the present Mr Darcy's father. I have just learned that the books were rediscovered and identified in the library of a private gentleman here in Hertfordshire, who bought them several years ago without knowing they had been stolen. If this gentleman can recognize and identify the Lieutenant as the one who sold him the stolen books, Mr Wickham could be brought before the magistrate. I believe transportation would be the sentence.

However, as I have said, England needs every man. I have connections, and I am certain you have as well, among the ranks of our sea-faring brethren. Are not several Marines employed on each convict ship to keep order? I would not strip our ranks of better qualified soldiers when we have one here who ought to have some disciplinary action, yet who is still capable of holding a musket and standing guard.

If you have leisure to do so tomorrow, Darcy and I would speak with you at Netherfield, and if possible, we would introduce you to Mr Bennet at Longbourn. I hope we can come to some agreeable decision regarding Lieutenant Wickham.

Respectfully,

Colonel Fitzwilliam

Twenty

10 November 1812

My papa is the horriblest man alive! It is the very worst thing ever. My poor Wickham! Papa says I may not leave the house today to "do something foolish and rash." As if I would ever! Send this note to Mrs Forster, for I was terribly fond of her, and we did have some good laughs at the Assembly. I know she will be of some help.

Miss Lydia Bennet to Mrs Andrew Forster

10 November 1812

I s it true? Oh, tell me it is not true that Mr Wickham has gone! We were all to be so merry at my aunt Philips to-morrow evening! You and Maria were to dance with all the officers, and I was to lean on Mr Wickham's arm as he played cards with all the gentlemen. Papa will tell me nothing but that my Wickham was blamed for stealing some stuffy old books or some rubbish. Who cares about books? Is my Wickham still in town? You must give him this note from me!

Miss Lydia Bennet to (the former) Lieutenant Wickham

The worst day of my life

(Note found crumpled in the barracks and burned to protect the ignorant)

O h, Wicky! I have cried my eyes out all day, but it is no good! My odious father says I am never to see you again! I do not know what happened. It is all the fault of that horrid Mr Darcy, for he and some colonel came to call on Papa this morning, then they were all off together with Colonel Forster and then this! But I have a plan. I shall sneak out of my room by night and come to the barracks. I am sure I can get the key from the guard, for do not the guards always fall asleep when they are guarding someone important? That is the way it always works in the best stories, and I am made of stout stuff. We shall escape to Paris and honeymoon on that big river Singe, or whatever it is.

Mr Thomas Bennet to Mr Edward Gardiner

10 November 1812

D ear Edward,

There is not a rational creature in the house today, so I have retreated to my library and taken up my pen. Even Mrs Bennet rarely disturbs me when I am writing, so I suppose you shall have a letter as I have reached the end of my nerves.

This morning, I received several young men at my door. The first was Collins, applying for Elizabeth's hand before my breakfast had even settled. I knew perfectly well what her answer would be, but I thought she might phrase it better than

I could, so I invited her down to do her own refusing. It was marvellous, for when he would not take her at her word, that mutt of hers expressed his opinion of the proposal. Oh, do not fear, the bite was only a superficial one and I doubt it will turn septic. But I daresay I shall be rid of my house guest within the week. He has gone off somewhere and has been absent all day, to which I sigh in relief.

Half an hour later, two carriages arrived, bearing seven more young men between them. I wondered if I had enough daughters to suit them all, but alas, it was not my daughters they came for. Not *only* my daughters, I should say, for one of them was decidedly an attraction, at least for Darcy. This was the first time he had left Netherfield since he arrived, and it is wonderful how that chap got about. He had left his Bath chair behind and was walking with the assistance of a cane. I say, I did not know his leg was so well healed as that, and I wondered if these last few weeks he has been keeping secrets to gain feminine sympathy. Well played, young man. He was in obvious discomfort and depended not a little on Bingley and another of the gentlemen, but he stood on his own two feet, nonetheless.

Lizzy is rarely lost for words, but she was on this day, particularly when Darcy walked over to her, nearly unaided, and kissed her hand when he thought no one was watching. I had not believed my second daughter quite so easily swayed by a member of the opposite sex, but it seems she can be as silly as the rest of them, given the proper inducement. A pity you declined the wager, for I should have liked a second bottle of Scotch.

Well, well, and now I come back to the reason for the carriages. It seems those old books of mine have come round to some further use. There is, or rather was, a lieutenant among the ranks of the militia who was some former connection of Darcy's. He was a great favourite with all the ladies in town, particularly my Lydia, who has sworn never to speak to me again. Let us hope she holds to that resolve for a day or two, for I could do with the peace and quiet. There is a deal to tell, so I shall endeavour to put it down logically.

Darcy and Bingley arrived in the first carriage with a Colonel Fitzwilliam—a jolly

and decentish fellow who, by all accounts, is single. Mrs Bennet is presently making inquiries. I spoke with Fitzwilliam while Darcy and Bingley found their way to two of my daughters. I shall let you guess which.

Shortly thereafter came the second carriage, bearing Colonel Forster of the local militia and Wickham, flanked by two guards. I say, I do not think he expected to be met with Darcy, or Colonel Fitzwilliam, for that matter, for all his bluster and charm vanished in an instant. He began to stammer and babble like a naughty boy, and well he might, for what awaits that blackguard shall not be pleasant.

It seems Wickham is the very man who sold me the stolen books some years ago. That was the purpose of their call, to see if I could place his face and show the books in my collection that had once belonged to the Darcy family. As it happened, I did not recall his face, but his voice, when I reflected on it, was the very one. After Wickham saw no escape and confessed to his crimes, the colonel was satisfied. I understand the former lieutenant will now be taking up guard duty on a prison hulk. I wonder that he is not to be counted among the prisoners himself, but perhaps there is some reprieve for the wicked, after all.

Since Darcy was there in my library, it was only the proper thing for me to offer to return his family's books. I knew quite well he would refuse, for he has his eye on an even greater treasure of mine. Mrs Bennet nearly asphyxiated herself with her handkerchief when Elizabeth gave Darcy her arm to steady him as he walked back to his carriage. She remained there with him far longer than I would have thought the gentleman could stand with comfort. I believe he likes her a little too well. She must return the regard, indeed, for she made Prince George mind his manners when he came to sniff Darcy's boots.

Now all at Longbourn is mayhem and fuss. Mrs Bennet is preparing an order of ribbons and lace that I shall have to cut in half if I am to afford it on the proceeds from this year's harvest and rents. Jane and Lizzy followed to Netherfield almost on the boot of the gentlemen's carriage, "to call on Miss Bingley and Miss Georgiana."

Mary is practicing her piano with renewed vigour because I understand Colonel Fitzwilliam expressed his admiration for a well-played tune. And Kitty and Lydia are presently weeping in their rooms, but I can still hear them from two floors down. I shall have a lock placed on Lydia's window before I retire for the night, because heaven only knows what schemes a girl more desperate than sensible may conceive.

I shall take a leisurely stroll to town now to post this letter. Perhaps by the time I return home, certain affairs will be settled, and I may again have peace in my library.

Thomas

Twenty-One

10 November 1812

F itzwilliam came to speak to me in my room this evening. He told me it is all settled with George Wickham. There, I can write his name again. But I shall not write more of him, because Miss Elizabeth said something the other day that I mean to put into practice: "Speak only of the past as its remembrance gives you pleasure." And so, I shall.

I am glad that chapter is closed. I feel as if I can breathe again and have some joy in anticipating the future again. Fitzwilliam is growing stronger each day, and he, too, said that he felt more optimistic about the morrow than he ever did in his life.

I believe he means to court Miss Elizabeth, and I am happy for him. I have never seen him smile as he does when she is near, and I think she is fond of him, too. At least, I have not seen her take such delight in bantering with anyone else as she does with him, and she has all of Harold's affections. What little affection that dog possesses, anyway.

Miss Bingley is in such a state whenever the Bennets come to call. We have been seeing them far more often than Lady Matlock says is fitting for proper callers, but no one but Miss Bingley and Mrs Hurst seems to care. Oh, how they carry on! Miss Bingley was so persuaded that my brother meant to marry her, though I cannot fathom where she got that notion. Fitzwilliam thinks she is little better than a peacock—gaudy and loud and a terrible nuisance to clean up after (I added that bit on my own, but I do think she would cause nothing but trouble in society).

I should not wonder if Mr Bingley and Miss Bennet also made a match of it, despite the harsh things Miss Bingley has to say behind their backs. She is terribly disappointed that her brother is not looking to London for his bride, and I even caught a hint that she wanted Mr Bingley to court *me* instead. But of course, that is ridiculous. I do not mean to court anyone for the rest of my life if I can help it.

But if I could find someone who looks at me the way Fitzwilliam looks at Elizabeth... perhaps I might change my mind.

Miss Elizabeth Bennet to Mrs Madeline Gardiner

27 November 1812

A unt,

I am speaking to Mr Darcy again.

Actually, I never ceased speaking to him, which was part of the trouble. Do you think two people who debate and argue for pure enjoyment can be said to truly get on? Because it is terribly fine sport, though we do cause some eyebrows to raise, and Mama is perpetually asking for her salts when she is in the room with us.

But I shall speak seriously for a moment. Let me mend my pen, so the ink looks the part.

Aunt Madeline, I may have taken leave of my senses. What would make me think that a man of Mr Darcy's situation in life would want me? He is a good man, but the best men are only as "good" as they are humble. I made that bit of wisdom up just now. What do you think of it?

Papa is a good man, but in my debates with Mr Darcy over books like *Peregrine Pickle*, I made an uncomfortable discovery about my family. Papa has been more often careless than prudent. I think that is a form of pride, is it not? For he would not trouble himself to any exertion beyond what he felt inclined to do. And Mr Collins and Marcus Danforth and Elliot Goulding—when they thought so well of themselves that they could not see the glaring personality defects that would make them terrible husbands? Pride, again. And laziness.

And Mr Wickham... oh, I have not told you all about Mr Wickham, but I saw Papa posting a fat letter to London last week, so perhaps he told you the whole tale. Mr Wickham was fetching when one first looked at him. But he turned out to be the prideliest of them all (I just invented that word, and I believe I shall file it to use again someday), for he made his way in the world through dishonesty and had no qualms about purposely injuring others.

So how do I think Mr Darcy is any different?

Well, he started off in my good graces for being so generous with his library. And he tugged at my sympathies for his predicament—I wanted to befriend the poor man, and he was so easy to write to, I naturally fell into something like friendship before I ever met him. Perhaps you might say I was prejudiced in his favour.

But I saw his true nature later—not when he thundered at us from the hall because he was out of temper that day, but when he poured out his soul in his letter of apology. A man not acquainted with humility could not honestly write what he wrote. Perhaps a practiced liar could, but I believe Mr Darcy's hair would all fall out, and his bones rot away if he tried to pass off a lie. He is not even capable of it. And all the pains he takes with his sister and his cousin, and yes, even that old dog of his, show what sort of heart he has. Yes, I do believe I can say that Mr Darcy is the best of men.

But that brings me back to my point. Aunt, I am in dire straits. What does it mean when your heart gallops like a racehorse and your skin prickles like goose flesh when a man smiles at you? Shall I send for the apothecary? Or should I just propose to him and have done with it? Because I have looked round, and my mind is quite made up. I want that one, please. And I hope he settles the matter first before I do something terribly shocking.

Your most ridiculously-in-love niece,
E

Lady Catherine de Bourgh to Lord Matlock

4 December 1812

B rother,
        I could have told you this would come. Yet here, at the end of all things, I find that not only are you silent, but that your own son is complicit in the affair!

Perhaps you are unaware that our nephew, our own nephew Darcy, has been in Hertfordshire since the middle of October? For nearly two months has he been languishing there, guest of a tradesman's son, ignoring his duties and passing himself off as lame when he is quite hale and, from what I can tell, sound and stubborn as he ever was. But I am ever attentive to these things.

My parson bears an unfortunate connection to a family in the area, as he will inherit a small estate. I advised him, as prudence would see fit, to seek himself a wife from among the daughters of his relative. I always desire a suitable outcome in these situations. But the chit to whom he proposed would not have him, and have you any idea why? Because she had got her head full of ideas far beyond her station!

Indeed, Darcy has been dallying with this disgraceful girl! Ignoring his obligations to Anne, what he owes society and his family, he has raised her expectations and claims he does not mean to come away. And she, with no notions of decency or propriety, stood before me this very afternoon and would not heed my demands!

I insist you speak to Darcy at once, for if you do not, I shall know how to act.

(Hereon affixed the great seal of)
Lady Catherine de Bourgh

Colonel Richard Fitzwilliam to the Earl of Matlock

5 December 1812

D ear Father,

No, I do not believe you will persuade Darcy to do anything but what he has already decided to do. I am sorry Lady Catherine was inconvenienced when she came but let me tell you how it happened and perhaps you will understand a bit of Darcy's resolve.

It is true that Darcy has his mind set on Miss Elizabeth Bennet. I could have told you that long before Lady Catherine. Darcy himself would have confessed it, for he makes no secret of his intentions—at least, not among ourselves. I do not believe he has spoken to Miss Elizabeth of them. They had a rather unconventional introduction, and though he is perfectly convinced of his feelings, he is not certain she is yet.

But that aside, Lady Catherine's behaviour the day before yesterday was... problematic. We had all finished a fine luncheon, and Darcy and Bingley and I had taken the carriage to town to call on Colonel Forster. We had recently concluded some business with the colonel and desired to maintain good-will, so to speak. While we were out, Lady Catherine came to Netherfield and found Georgiana in the drawing room with Miss Bingley. Oh, to clarify, Miss Bingley has no generous feelings toward Miss Elizabeth. That complicated matters.

I am not sure of all the details, but apparently, Lady Catherine berated poor Georgiana until she cried, and all for doing nothing more than being in the room when Darcy was not. Then Miss Bingley put in her bit. Apparently, she made it sound as if Darcy were somehow accused of compromising Miss Elizabeth, and this supposed attachment was merely the wiles of a fortune hunter. There was nothing in it, she claimed, and if Lady Catherine would but persuade her nephew to return to London, all would be forgotten.

Lady Catherine left at once to swoop down upon Long-bourn and the hapless Miss Elizabeth. I know not how that conversation played out, save that both were apparently in-censed afterwards. Lady Catherine flogged her carriage back to Netherfield, spitting fire all the way. This time, she found Darcy and ticked his last nerve. Father, Darcy raised his voice to her! I would never have believed it, but I was in the room when it happened.

After Lady Catherine left—unsatisfied, mind you—Darcy called for a carriage to take him to Longbourn at once. I thought surely it would bring him to the point and they would settle things between them at last, but when he came back, he said nothing of what happened. I was left to glean gossip, which was spare. All anyone knows is that Miss Elizabeth was indignant at Lady Catherine's accusations of playing the coquette, and that she told Darcy she didn't need to "snag a husband to hide some imaginary shame."

Well, there you have it all. Please do something about Lady Catherine, for if you or Mother do not, Darcy might. And by the look in his eye today, I would pity my aunt if she crossed him again.

Fondly,
Richard

Miss Elizabeth Bennet to Mrs Charlotte Collins

4 December 1812

Dear Charlotte,

Kent sounds lovely, but I just met your Lady Catherine de Bourgh and found her far from ladylike. Perhaps you ought to burn this note before your new husband reads it.

Her arrogance, I can suffer. What I cannot abide is the presumption that I have poached Mr Darcy's affections by shameful means. How did such a report spread so far? I can tell you the answer, though you may not like it.

Whatever anyone else says or thinks, I have done nothing to lure Mr Darcy into a compromise! I suppose taken in the wrong light, all the letters we sent were… no, I still say it was innocent. Anyone who thinks otherwise is a fool. His honour and my virtue are unsullied.

I never swooned in my life, but I swoon now whenever I hear his voice. Oh, Charlotte, what shall I do if he does not love me as I adore him? I feel as if I have been half a being my whole life until now. But Lady Catherine was right about one thing: he is out of my sphere.

How shall I be content if everyone presumes that someone like Mr Darcy would only have someone like me if I had tricked him and disgraced myself? I would sooner not marry at all than have that over my head for the rest of my life. Indeed, I was jesting with you before you left and in my last letter to my aunt Gardiner that if Darcy did not propose to me, I might take on the duty for him, but I did not mean it in *that* way!

I think.

He came here this afternoon to apologize on behalf of his aunt, but he said nothing of love. Nor did I. I think we were both too shaken and mortified to consider speaking of something like that. And also, Mama was in hysterics, and Lydia and Kitty were making such a scene—I know you can well imagine. If Mr Darcy has any sense, there will be no cause to worry about Lady Catherine's accusations because he will take himself—and my heart—back to Derbyshire and stay there, where he is safe.

I think I will go eat all the sweets in the larder now.

Ever your fondest friend,
Lizzy

Twenty-Two

Miss Jane Bennet to Mrs Madeline Gardiner

9 December 1812

Dear Aunt Madeline,

I am sorry to hear the children all have colds. We were so hoping to see you this week for Christmas, but of course, you cannot travel with sick children, and they need their mother at home. I hope they recover soon.

Aunt, I have the most wonderful news. Mr Bingley has asked me to marry him! He came this morning, first to speak to me and then to Papa. I know his sisters do not approve of me, and that pains me some, but I shall have ample sources of pleasure in him. Charles is the dearest and kindest man alive, and I know we will be terribly happy.

But I feel badly for Lizzy.

I suppose she has told you something of how she feels about
Mr Darcy. Aunt, they cannot be in a room together, but they
somehow find one another and talk as if they were the only
two people in the world. And if they are separated, it has
become a joke between Papa and me that Lizzy and Darcy are
watching each other every moment until they can be beside
each other again. But Mr Darcy did not come with Charles
today.

I cannot think why unless he does not mean to make her
an offer after all. Could that be true? It is clear how much
he admires her, but can he truly mean to marry someone of
finer circles? Charles told me Mr Darcy often counselled him
to marry prudently, and perhaps he is waiting for a wife who
can add to Pemberley's coffers. If that is true, my heart breaks
for Lizzy. Would you mind writing to her to lend her some
encouragement? I feel I can offer little at present.

Mama says to ask you if we might come to stay for a few days
to shop for my trousseau. Naturally, we would wait until after
Twelfth Night, and I would hope by then the children might
be well. But if you can, ~

Aunt, since I wrote the above, the strangest thing has happened! I looked out the window to see a tremendous carriage
pulling up to the gate, and a very fine lady got out. I hastened
downstairs with everyone else to find out who she was. She
introduced herself as Lady Matlock, come all the way from
London this morning, and she asked to speak with Elizabeth.
Alone.

The last time this happened, we all heard every word because Lady Catherine's voice carried, and Elizabeth was an-
grier than I had ever seen her. But Lady Matlock was quiet
and, dare I say it, very much like I pictured a fine lady. They
retired to Papa's study instead of walking in the garden as she
had with Lady Catherine, because it is snowing. They spoke
for full half an hour. They even rang for tea. And then Lady

Matlock left, back for London. She would not even stop for the day but meant to return home this very afternoon.

What could it mean? I asked Lizzy, but she seemed like a girl in a trance. She hardly spoke a word to anyone, though Mama imagined all sorts of things. Papa finally told everyone to let Lizzy be, and I am glad because she looked as if one callous word could shatter her. No, she was not precisely sad. Nor happy. Anxious, perhaps, and intensely focused on her thoughts. All she told me was that Lady Matlock was Mr Darcy's other aunt (Colonel Fitzwilliam's mother) and that they had a pleasant conversation.

Well, I do not know what to think. But as I look out my window now, I am not shocked to see (and nor should you be to hear of it) Lizzy traipsing across the snowy fields toward Netherfield. I see Prince George following her, and she is walking in such a way to outpace a Thoroughbred.

Perhaps tomorrow there will be more news. Or a scandal. It could be either, I suppose, but I will seal this letter now so you may spend time speculating like the rest of us.

With love,
Jane

Colonel Richard Fitzwilliam to the Earl and Countess of Matlock

9 December 1812

D ear Father and Mother,

   Whatever you both did, it worked. However, I wonder at Mother for coming all this way and never stopping at
Netherfield! I did not know she had come until... well, I am
sure you want the complete story in sequence.

I told you Darcy was morose after Lady Catherine's visit.
Georgiana was terrified, Miss Elizabeth was offended, and
Darcy hardly knew what to say to either of them. I do not think
Darcy and Miss Bennet had seen each other since he went to
apologize for Lady Catherine's effrontery, but I know he put
on his boots every day as if he meant to go somewhere. I think
he simply did not know how to undo this kerfuffle without
making it worse, and he was in mortal terror of losing Miss
Elizabeth's regard entirely.

I do not think she was ever put out with Darcy himself.
From what I have overheard, she felt embarrassed by other
people's assumptions. I doubt any woman likes being told
she is so far beneath her beloved that she could only have
ensnared him by unjust means. But I can tell you, and I am
certain Mother has seen, that Miss Elizabeth is a girl of intelligence and quality. Oh, she sports with people more than most
would consider dignified. That is one of the reasons Darcy fell
so hard for her—she is reflective and intellectual like him, but
she refuses to let him be serious for too long. And you know
how he can turn grave and silent if left to his own devices.

He was in such a mood this afternoon. Bingley was over the
moon with his betrothal to Miss Jane Bennet (perhaps I have
not told you there was another match in the offing), and he
had gone off to give his sisters the news. I doubt they were
pleased, but we did not overhear that conversation. I was in
the drawing room, listening to Georgie play the piano while
Darcy brooded by the window with that old dog of his. You
can always tell when Darcy is in a gloomy temper because
Harold will not leave his side.

But then he jumped up as if stung by a bee. "By heaven!" he exclaimed and fairly galloped out of the room with the dog at his heels. Georgie and I were left staring at each other and shrugging, but then we saw Darcy race by the window. We ran to the glass ourselves to see what the matter was. Incidentally, that is the first time Darcy has run since before his accident, and he fared better than I expected.

Would you imagine it? Miss Elizabeth had walked all the way from Longbourn, in the snow, her skirts six inches deep in frost and ice! She must have been freezing by the time she arrived, but she did not act like it. And because Georgie and I are shameless, we pushed open the window so we might hear what she came to say.

"Do you regret our introduction? All those letters we exchanged?" she demanded of him. (Perhaps I will explain that in a different letter.)

"What? Never! They were a life line to me." was his response.

"Do you think me too bold and forward? Do you find me too impertinent?"

Darcy took a step closer to her. "Impossible. Why would you ask such things?"

"Because I mean to prove you wrong."

And then she did something that made me cover Georgiana's eyes. Aye, she leapt into his arms and kissed him, there before God and everyone—well, anyone who happened to be looking out the window. Which, so far as I know, was only Georgie and me. It is a wonder she did not knock him down, for he has not his full strength yet, but he caught her quite admirably. I shall not describe what else we saw, for it is not fitting for a polite letter.

Well, after that, I suppose Darcy *was* trapped in a compromise, but not for a second would he complain. In fact, I never knew Darcy had so many teeth, but they have all been on display this afternoon. I almost did not recognize him with such an expression on his face.

If Mother had formerly given her stamp of approval to Miss Elizabeth's character and is now rethinking that assessment, I beg her to give it time. They will be ridiculous for a while, in company and in private, then they may come to be rational again. At least sometimes.

My usefulness here seems to be at an end, so I mean to come to you at the end of the week for the remainder of my leave. I return to the Continent the first week of February, but Darcy has promised me I will stand up at his wedding before I go. I believe there is less excitement in Portugal at present than there is here, and I am looking forward to the rest.

Richard

Miss Elizabeth Bennet to Mrs Charlotte Collins

9 December 1812

C harlotte,
        Lady Catherine appears to me a woman who will not countenance disappointment. So, I did not disappoint her.

I am a hoyden. A temptress and a tart, too, it seems, and utterly unrepentant. I am, after all, the girl who spent the summer writing most improper letters to an unmarried gentleman. I must act the part.

Lady Matlock came to call on me today. I was bracing myself for another attack on my morals and my character and the very fact that I am drawing air from this earth that could have been devoted to someone of higher rank. Alas, I was disappointed, for she was polite. The colonel, her son, had written to her as well as Lady Catherine, and she determined to come to Hertfordshire and meet me for herself to determine which of them had me pegged.

Her judgment was neither. I was not half so innocent as the colonel presumed, but I was no fanged beast, either. She did not meet Prince George. While I cannot say she thought I was the loveliest girl she ever met—that honour belongs to a Miss Emmaline, daughter of Lord Walton—she did not forbid me from marrying her nephew. I was almost disappointed in that, because I had been starting to think that the forbidden things in life taste the sweetest. She also said that she could see precisely why her nephew was in love with me, and that I "would probably not disgrace him."

Well, she was wrong in that last bit, for I managed it in a single day, but... he was in love with me? Not merely friendly fascination that can lead nowhere, but so much in love that he has upset his noble relatives for fear he would actually marry me? Lady Catherine is barking mad, but Lady Matlock... if she says it, it must be so. I did not know how she learned this, but I set out at once for Netherfield to find out if it was true.

It was.

I have decided to kiss Fitzwilliam—yes, he is mine now—every time he goes out of doors in the winter. There is something intoxicating about biting cold air and warm, steamy breath and his soft kiss and strong arms picking me up from the snow. Indeed, Charlotte, he picked me up! The man who almost never walked again! Granted, he stumbled somewhat.

Actually, he fell. We both did, but I found out I can assault him just as well from the ground. Perhaps better. I think today was the first time he did not curse that half-healed leg of his.

Did you know he has very *large* hands? I mean to find out what they can do. (I told you I was a hoyden.)

We were a sight when we came indoors. Colonel Fitzwilliam called for a maid to hasten me into a bedroom and defrost my hair before anyone else saw us. Georgiana was giggling uproariously, and I think I have proved a poor influence on that girl already. I am only getting started.

You may want to accidentally drop this letter in the cook stove, too, because it is probably for the best that your husband has a week or two of peace before everyone hears our latest scandal. And now, I must go downstairs and tell Mama, for I was too excited to speak to anyone but Jane when I first returned home.

On second thought, it will do you no good to burn this. Once Mama hears, the whole world will, for there is nothing that travels faster than the post.

You must come visit us at Pemberley in the spring.
Your most loving and deliriously happy,
Lizzy

Epilogue

Mrs Elizabeth Darcy to Mrs Madeline Gardiner

12 February 1813

M y dearest aunt,

Pemberley is everything you said it would be, and then more. Papa will simply die when he sees the library! I would go on and on about its many splendours, but I am too content to do anything but dawdle with my pen and admire my husband as he sits by the firelight.

He encouraged me to tend to my letters, as he was quite taken with you and my uncle and desires me to invite you and the children to Pemberley as soon and as often as it is convenient. But I confess, I am not much in the mood for writing. It is difficult to write a long letter unless I can put down something cheeky, and I am feeling far too mellow for that sort of thing.

I have every source of happiness here. Fitzwilliam and I suit. I do not know how to say it better than that, though it lacks description and imagination. We simply are... like one. Indeed, we are both stubborn, and I am certain we shall quarrel—we do already, but that is for amusement rather than actual discord. But where there is respect and admiration and true similarity of character, I believe quarrels must only bring us closer together in the end. There, that is my bit of wisdom after only a month of marriage. Time will tell if I am correct.

This night, however, I fear you will have only a brief note, for my mind is more agreeably engaged. Did you know I married such a handsome man? I find it enjoyable simply to look on his face when he does not know it. But it is even more delightful to nestle in his arms and read a book together or venture out for short rambles around the park when the weather permits. Yes, Fitzwilliam's leg is fully recovered from his ordeal, and he is... quite a vigorous man. If I dare put something like that on paper. I suppose I found something cheeky to say, after all.

He and I danced this evening for the first time. Georgiana played a gentle tune for us, and my husband offered me his hand. Aunt, I said yes, and I shall say yes, every day forever. And then we went for a walk in the orangery, my husband and I, with Harold and Prince George as chaperons, to be certain we did nothing indiscreet. Apparently, there is some fear among the household that we ought not to be disturbed if we should happen to be in a room alone together.

That is all I had to write, but I shall answer your question before I seal my letter. You asked me when I felt sure of my feelings for Mr Darcy. I would say it was when he first looked up from his Bath chair and smiled at me.

Ever yours,

Elizabeth Marie Darcy
(I do like how my new name looks all written out.)

Private Diary of Fitzwilliam Darcy

9 December 1813

I have neglected my diary for some while. The reason, naturally, is that I have since discovered a far more agreeable ear to whisper my secrets and my doubts into than this blank page in my journal. I may give up keeping a diary entirely, for I would far rather hold Elizabeth than my pen. But today, my life changed, and I feel as if I must shout it to the heavens.

Today, I held my son as he took his first breaths. And perhaps it is fitting, for when I look at the date, it is the very anniversary of the day when my Elizabeth marched across the wintry pastures round Netherfield and claimed me for her own—the day I myself came to life. When my courage failed, hers rose. Since that day, we have found that often to be the case—one is always the other's strength through weakness.

A year and a half ago, it was I who depended on her for cheer and heart. Without realizing why I was so drawn to her letters and later to her person, I was sustained by her wit, her humour, and the tender concern I felt in her words.

But today, it was I who carried her when the pains of childbirth must have nearly ripped her in two. Oh, what I would have done to take that agony for her! All I could do was bear her upstairs when it all came upon her, and to hold her hand when her strength was nearly spent. No, I did not permit myself to be sent away, as any decent husband would do. And for that, she rewarded me with a smile, a caress to my cheek, and a kiss to my brow as we beheld our son together for the first time.

Elizabeth is resting now, and I have still not left her side. Neither have the dogs. They are not yet permitted in the room, but they are scratching at the door. Tomorrow, I will let them to her, when Harold's weight on the blankets beside her will not cause her discomfort and Prince George's antics on the floor will amuse her rather than wake her from much-needed slumber.

Of anyone, I ought to know how exhausting and yet how dull it is to simply wait for one's body to heal. And so, I shall be here for her. Be it with a book to read together, with a letter to laugh or sigh over, or just putting my arms around her when she wants to rest, she will not be left to recover alone.

Such an odd turn of fate! I can still hardly believe that a stack of stolen books and a mistaken letter could have brought her into my life. But I thank God for her each day. For her fine eyes and sparkling smile, her gentle touch when I am low, and her bubbling laugh when I am merry. For the enchanting twist she can put on even the mundane things of life, and the stout faith she holds in me, whether or not I deserve it.

My life would be worth nothing, had not this dear and lovely Hertfordshire lass the impertinence to introduce herself to a stranger in a letter.

K

eep smiling with more fun and flirty Darcy and Elizabeth romance! Pick up your copy of *Mr. Darcy Steals a Kiss* today!

From Alix

Thank you for indulging with me and spending a little time with Darcy and Elizabeth.

I hope you've had a delightful escape to Pemberley. I'd love it if you would share this family with your friends so they can experience a love to last for the ages. As with all my books, I have enabled lending to make it easier to share. If you leave a review for *A Proper Introduction* on Amazon, Goodreads, Book Bub or your own blog, I would love to read it! Email me the link at **Author@AlixJames.com.**

Would you like to read more of Darcy and Elizabeth's romance? I have an emotional rollercoaster for you to try next! Dive into *Mr. Darcy Steals a Kiss* or *London Holiday*. Laugh along with our favorite couple as they find the love they were destined for!

And if you're hungry for more, including a free ebook of satisfying short tales, stay up to date on upcoming releases and sales by joining my newsletter: https://dashboard.maile rlite.com/forms/249660/73866370936211000/share

About Alix James

Short and satisfying romance for busy readers.

Alix James is an alternate pen name for best-selling Austenesque author Nicole Clarkston.

Always on the go as a wife, mom, and small business owner, she rarely has time to read a whole novel. She loves coffee with the sunrise and being outdoors. When she does get free time, she likes to read, camp, dream up romantic adventures, and tries to avoid housework.

Each Alix James story is a clean Regency Variation of approximately 20,000 words.

Visit her website and sign up for her newsletter at Alix James | (nicoleclarkston.com)

Also By Alix James

Classic Pride and Prejudice Variations

These Dreams

Nefarious

Tempted

Darcy and Elizabeth: Heart to Heart Collection

The Rogue's Widow
London Holiday

The Courtship of Edward Gardiner

London Holiday

Rumours and Recklessness

Darcy and Elizabeth: Sweet Escapes Collection

<u>North and South Variations</u>

Nowhere but North

Northern Rain

No Such Thing as Luck

John and Margaret: Coming Home Collection

<u>Anthologies</u>

Rational Creatures

Falling for Mr Thornton

<u>Spanish Translations</u>

Rumores e Imprudencias

Vacaciones en Londres

Nefasto

Un Compromiso Accidental

Reina del Invierno

Una Mente Noble

<u>Italian Translations</u>

Una Vacanza a Londra

<u>The Short and Sassy Series:</u>

Unintended

Spirited Away

Indisposed

Love and Other Machines

Elizabeth Bennet: Short and Sassy Compilation

The Sweet Sentiments Series:

When the Sun Sleeps

Cuando el Sol se Duerm (Spanish Translation)

Queen of Winter

Reina del Invierno (Spanish Translation)

A Fine Mind

Una Mente Noble (Spanish translation)

The Frolic and Romance Series:

A Proper Introduction

A Good Memory is Unpardonable

Along for the Ride

The Mr. Darcy Series:

Mr. Darcy Steals a Kiss

Mr. Darcy and the Governess